# Unmistakably Yours

Nini Lester

Moonlight & Pen Publishing

Published by Moonlight & Pen Publishing
United States of America
For permissions or inquiries, contact:
Moonlightandpen@gmail.com

Editorial Services: Black Girls Who Edit, an editorial agency by Black Girls Who Write, LLC.

Cover Art by Sonicah Sanon | Logo Art by Joyus Creationz

First Edition: April 2026

ISBN: 979-8-9949923-0-2 (Paperback)
ISBN: 979-8-9949923-2-6 (Hardback)

*Drink water and call your sistas*

## Author's Note

This is a work of fiction, but it's stitched with truth, like a beautiful tapestry. Some parts were imagined; others lived. The story was written for healing—for understanding, for forgiveness, and for love that grows even through pain.

If you see yourself in one of these pages, know that's intentional. Sometimes fiction is how we give voice to what couldn't be said aloud, and what feels familiar is meant to be recognized, felt, and honored.

I also wrote this story with love; for Black love, for the quiet strength that carries us, and for the moments that teach us how to begin again, for the moments we allow ourselves to be vulnerable. I hope that wherever you are on your journey; you find softness, ease, and peace within these pages, just as I have in writing them. Please note, this story also contains themes of grief and the loss of a loved one. It also contains consensual on page intimacy between adults.

**Haitian Creole Phrases**

Throughout this book, you'll find Haitian Creole phrases woven into dialogue and  narration. I've included their meanings here to offer context as you read.

*Antouka* — Anyways; regardless; in any case

*Tèt chaje* —That's a lot; that's overwhelming


*Ou pa wont?* — You not ashamed?!

*Chérie* — Darling; sweetheart

# CHAPTER ONE
## *Mia*

I'm standing in the restaurant bathroom, staring at my reflection, trying to decide how much lying I'm willing to do tonight. A sudden migraine is believable. Stomach unwell after a few bites—a bit dramatic but effective. I could even text my sister, Destiny, to call me with an emergency; like a pipe burst at the shop. I rinse my hands even though they aren't dirty to give myself thirty more seconds to come up with a plan. My date, Mark, is obnoxious, though he didn't come off that way at all when we met at my shop but it's clear as day now. Right as the appetizers came out he smirked and asked. *"Are you flexible?".*

I looked at him sideways, one brow lifting. "Excuse me?" He half-laughed, clearly pleased with himself. "I really love for the women I'm dating to be open minded".

I had no idea where he thought that conversation was headed, I just knew not a single part of me was going with it. I fluff my curls, smooth my dress, take a breath and head back to the table. He's mid-chew when I sit down. Mouth open. Fully committed. I don't know if his drinks are getting to him or if he's naturally this sloppy.

"So, is the flower business you run with your sister all your doing? Or do you have a long term business strategy?" he asks me.

"Tuh!" air expels out my nose as I half laugh without humor.

*Let me get the fuck up outta here, thank God I drove.*

"Excuse me, I have to go." I respond without answering his question.

I wave the waiter down and signal with my hand for the check.

"Done already?" he asks, looking genuinely confused. "We haven't been here long, and you barely touched your food!"

"Yeah, my stomach is upset all of a sudden." It's like he ignored what I said. Right as I finish my sentence he leans across the table, with his fingers still greasy, and attempts to touch my hair.

I pull back and my eyes grow wide. "Don't". I say sternly.

He blinks surprised. "Relax," he starts. "I'm just loving that hair!"

The waiter comes seconds after and places the bill on the table before I can open my mouth again.

"Soo...split the bill?"

Did this fool really just ask to *"split the bill?"*

I don't say a word, just slap my card on the table, relieved that our time together was coming to an end. I should've trusted my intuition. I suspected his world and mine wouldn't align from the jump. Before this date he seemed kind, and I didn't think he was bad looking considering Caucasian men normally aren't my ministry.  But I did feel there was a disconnect between us as we chatted over the phone. I came to the date to be open and clearly that was a mistake.

Hell, I knew this date was over as soon as I saw he showed up in flip flops.

*Why do men do shit like that?*

The kind of love I see for myself is with a man who understands what it means to move through the world the way I do—someone aligned with both my worldview and life experience. Sure, growing up in a Haitian household is unique in its own way, but still. Being raised by a Black-Haitian mother teaches you to move through the world with a different kind of awareness. It's taught me pride, resilience, and how to embrace ease. As things were so different for her. Survival came first, desire came later. There wasn't much room for dreaming, only enduring. I have the chance to choose differently and avoid settling. I've built this life for myself, I don't need a man to complete it.

The receipts are brought back and I sign so fast my signature comes out like a scribble. I grab my bag and head to the door not checking for him but he follows me outside, like the evening hasn't already expired. The night air hits my face and as peaceful as it is, his footsteps behind me won't allow me to enjoy it. I feel my aggravation flare.

"Well, I know it was short but I had a great time with you. Text me when you get home babe," he adds, smiling like he earned something. " I roll my eyes again and get in my Lexus.

"Goodbye, Mark," I reply in a curt tone.

He blows me a kiss as he starts to walk away but I don't acknowledge it. My expression is stale. Without another word, I just shut my door. Alicia Keys' *Diary* album fills my car and I drive off anticipating how my body will melt once I land in bed.

*

*BEEEP. BEEEP. BEEEP—*

I wake up startled, hand scrambling under the covers to find my phone and shut off the alarm. I press the side button until the beeping stops, then sink deeper into the coziness of my blankets. Damn. 7:00 a.m. came with a quickness. Just five more minutes. I toss over, rub my eyes and check my phone and see a text and a frown takes over my face.

*Mark: Good morning, beautiful. Last night was great. When can I take you out again?*

I read the message once, then twice. Could he even call it "taking me out" since he made me split the bill?

*Me: Actually, Mark, I'm not interested, but take care of yourself and have a great rest of your week.*

Bubbles. Immediately.

*Mark: Can I ask why? I felt like we really had a connection?*
For a moment, I hesitate with my response; I stare at the question, amazed by the audacity.

*Mark: Don't tell me it's because I split the bill...Listen, women these days take us high-value men for granted. It's only fair I get to know you first before I invest. In fact, you should respect that.*

I rub my eyes, making sure I'm reading his text correctly. No this mothafucka didn't. When the telltale sign of bubbles reappears in the chat. *He's still going?*

Blocked.

I drop my phone back onto my nightstand and lazily toss and turn in bed for a few more minutes before finally peeling myself up, each movement a struggle against the pull of exhaustion. The room is still quiet. The deep navy walls of my room soak up the early light streaming in from the windows, and the woven lanterns overhead cast a soft golden glow across the floor. Tall plants—the kind that don't ask for much—fill most of the room's corners. Lord knows I've never been the best plant mom, but I'm trying to change that, because someday I would like to maintain a big backyard with an established garden where I grow most of my own food.

I walk into my bathroom to start my morning routine and the smell of coffee drifts in as I brush my teeth. My little sister, Destiny, is already up, and since she makes the best coffee, my first thought is *Damn, I hope she saved me some.* I finish my skincare routine and head to the kitchen where Lana Del Rey echoes through the house—a good indicator that Destiny's probably in the middle of doing her aerial silks again.

"Hey, suga! Feed the cats for me?" she calls out as I pass her mid-pose. I glance up to see her long slender body hanging from her silks effortlessly, twisting into something both delicate and strong. The cut of the ceiling makes her look even higher up than she really is. Sunlight beams through the tall arched windows of our living room, scattering rainbows around her honey brown skin, her dark brown tiny coils bouncing around her face as she flows in the air. She scrunches her nose just a little when she transitions into the next hold. Destiny has always moved as though gravity is just a suggestion, making every practice session in our home look like a grand performance.

"Yeah, I got it. Tell me you left me some coffee?" I search the counter.

"In the microwave!" she shouts down to me, not missing a beat as she begins to descend gracefully from several feet in the air.

"You're the best," I grin, grabbing my cup. Destiny grabs her cup on the counter and leans against it, she playfully squints her almond shaped dark brown eyes and has a sly smile, filled with curiosity.

"So...how'd the date go?" she inquires delicately. I groan, rolling my eyes.

"Ugh...I don't even know why I went. I knew I wasn't feeling our conversation much over the phone." Destiny's lips twitch into a knowing smile.

"Oh, no...Was he all surface level? Lacking depth? Too monotonous?"

"Bingo," I say, taking a sip of my coffee. I reach for my small pill organizer by the sink for my birth control, swallowing one absentmindedly before continuing. "And with greasy fingers that he tried to touch my hair with, to top it all off." I wrinkle my nose before continuing. "He was just giving this classic finance-bro energy and acted like our shop wasn't a real thing. And then, of course, when I started to break things off over text this morning, he had the nerve to drop in some egotistical remark about being a 'high-value man.'" I roll my eyes. Destiny laughs.

"Ewww, get him away from us! Why do men keep listening to these stupid red-pill podcasts? It's asinine and baffles me that they don't hear how ridiculous they sound."

"It really is so ridiculous, I don't know why so many men are consuming it—it's brain rot, really." I lean back on the counter, feeling the peacefulness of the kitchen wrap around me.

"Well, cheers to dodging another inept man who thinks ego matters more than character." I clink my mug against hers.

"My angels must be working overtime." I pause and look over at my sister, who might as well be an angel in her own right.

Destiny has always been the most vibrant of us three sisters—there's a spark that sets her apart. It's as if she carries the sun within her, always flowing with warmth and creativity. Being around her always leaves me uplifted and inspired. After our mom passed three years ago, Destiny summoned up the courage to quit her job—which she'd earned a master's degree in biological sciences for—and moved to San Diego to become a full-time artist and small business co-owner.

Mom and Destiny's relationship was complicated. At times, our mother controlled every move Destiny made, even down to what she ate. My mom's reasoning was because she's the youngest, she didn't explain further than that. When she passed, it was as if Destiny was reborn while navigating her grief, discovering unknown parts of herself in the midst of it all. And it just so happened that her talent bloomed well beyond just painting, but into stained glass, jewelry, and copper art too. Her Etsy shop and market appearances have been nothing short of successful, even when she's downplayed them. It was at one of these very events that she was recently discovered by a curator working for an internationally renowned art gallery, which in turn, led to her being invited to participate in their next showing in Paris, France.

In the beginning of our shared business journey, outside commitments like these meant that I had to take on a lot of extra shifts, but business has thankfully grown enough that we've been able to hire a few additional staff, including our invaluable shift lead, José.

"Are you riding with me this morning?" I ask her.

"Nope! Bryan's picking me up. We're gonna hit the beach before I clock in at the shop. José is opening, so I won't be in until around noon."

"Perfect. By the way, I'm going to pick up some wine for sister night at the end of the week."

"Okay, sounds like a plan. Text me before you go to the store, though, so I can send you a small list."

Back in my room, I slip into my pink gym 'fit. *Might as well look cute today,* I think, *so I can shake off the bad vibes from last night.* I hop in my car, blast the AC, and let J. Cole fill the space.

The ten-minute drive to the gym flies by. This used to be a pretty quiet town. Thanks to the petting zoo up the road featuring its goats and alpacas on Instagram nonstop, and also the vintage aesthetic shops lining the streets with their hidden treasures and trinkets, this town is all over people's feeds now. It's still charming, but much harder to find stillness here these days. Before exiting the car, I grab my water bottle and check my watch—7:30 a.m. *I need to be out by 8:15 to make it to the shop by 8:30, so there's no time to waste,* I prepare myself mentally.

The musky smell of sweat hits me as soon as I walk in, and it almost makes me gag. The truth is, I don't exactly love coming to the gym but I can't deny that after a workout, I feel good not just physically, but mentally. I shake my head to get rid of the feeling and head straight for the treadmill, cranking the speed and letting the incline rise. Thankfully, my adrenaline kicks in almost immediately. I take off, pushing myself into the day ahead.

*

"Iced Empress Tea!" José calls out, lifting the drink above the counter. At his announcement, a couple of customers glance up from their phones. A woman sporting a red blazer and a headset—likely in the middle of a work call—steps forward with a grateful smile, silently accepting the drink as he hands it over. José has become such an integral part of this shop; he joined us just six months after we opened and soon after we promoted him to manager. He handles all of our social media marketing, and supports us with ordering and replenishing our tea and coffee inventory, all while juggling school part-time. Truly, this shop wouldn't be what it is today without him. He's holding it down as always on the cafe side while I focus on a customer's floral arrangements.

"Here you go, Iesha," I say, setting a full-bodied finished bouquet of pink roses, a variety of ranunculus flowers, velvety dahlias, red eucalyptus, and a few dusty rose-colored peonies. "I kept the inspiration suggestions you sent over in mind but made a few small tweaks I think you'll love." Iesha leans in, eyes wide.

"Oh my goodness, Mia, this is gorgeous. It'll be perfect for the grand table at my charity event tonight."

"I'm glad to hear it!" I say. "We had a few extra peonies in bloom this season, so I added in a couple of those too. It felt like the perfect finishing touch."

"It *is* perfect," she agrees, bringing the arrangement close to her face to smell it. We exchange payment, and without me even asking or mentioning it, she snaps a quick photo before tagging our shop on Instagram. A humble smile tugs at my lips.

Before I can say anything more, the front door swings open and in comes Destiny, right at 12:00 p.m. on the dot.

"Hey!" she calls out cheerfully, stepping inside like a sunbeam.

"Hey!" "Hi!" José and I both chime in at once. Destiny heads behind the counter and drops her bag.

"José! I *love* the photos you posted on our Instagram—they look amazing," she says.

"Of course, Destiny," José says, grinning. "You know I love playing photographer, boo, that's my jam."

"It really is! Also, how are your classes going?"

"Really well! I've got an exam coming up pretty soon but I've been studying plenty, so I think I'll do fine."

"Let us know if you need any time off to prep," Destiny replies sincerely.

"Absolutely," I add. "We've got you."

"Thank you both, I love y'all hoes," he says with a smirk.

"We love you more," I say, smiling at him.

After our three-way exchange, we each drift toward our respective corners and lock onto our tasks. The traffic of our shop moves around us with the scent of fresh-baked cookies on one side, the perfume of flowers on the other, and the gentle clinking of mugs in the space between. I take it all in, my heart full. This little world we've built is so much more than just a shop, I think to myself proudly.

*It's our legacy.*

# CHAPTER TWO
## *Khalid*

The loud buzzing of my phone startles me awake. I pat around until I find it—half-buried under my pillow—and raise the screen to my face to see an incoming FaceTime call: *Sharie.*

I stare at the screen for a second before answering. It's my first day off from work since I made my temporary move from Florida to California for my travel nurse contract. It would be nice to sleep in, hell I'm hardly adjusted, but the guilt of dodging her calls all week since leaving Florida gets to me.

The second I hit accept, I regret it.

"Hello?" My voice is hoarse, sleep still clinging to it. Sharie's face fills my screen like she's right in front of me, her eyes already sharp.

"So you really weren't gonna call me? It's been a whole week already since you got to Cali and you already acting brand new," she snaps.

My throat tightens. It'd be easier to apologize, I know—but I don't owe her that. I don't have feelings for her anymore, I remind myself—and I haven't in a long time. This thing we've been pretending is a friendship is anything but.

"Sharie, it's still early here and it's my first day off. I've been working four twelves back-to-back. I haven't even settled in yet."

"Uh huh," she says, rolling her eyes. "You act like you can't text. Do you have your schedule for next month yet?"

"No," I answer quickly, already knowing where this is going.

Sharie and I haven't been together for awhile. I broke things off with her for good nearly three months ago, but the boundaries between us remained blurred—a favor here, a guilt trip there, another fight to reel me back in...

"Well, how do your days off work then?" she presses.

"I don't know yet, Sharie. Like I said, I've only been here for barely a week."

"Why are you acting so disrespectful? I'm just trying to see when I'm supposed to come visit and you're being real short like we didn't just get on the phone after a whole week of not speaking."

"Disrespectful?" I echo, confusion in my voice. I take a deep breath and try again. "Honestly, Sharie, I'm not even sure it's for the best that you—" The words slip out before I can catch them. I brace myself.

"Excuse me?!" Her tone carries emphasis in every syllable. "So now you're saying you don't want me to come see you?" Attitude saturates each word.

"No, Sharie, I'm sorry—I just...I don't think it's a good idea. For either of us."

For a moment, there's silence, but not the peaceful kind. It's the kind that builds before it explodes. Old arguments replay in my mind like the songs of a greatest-hits album. The yelling, the obscene insults, the name calling...shit, every other week I was a "bitch." She wore her pettiness like a joke—playful until it wasn't and when it hurt others such as myself, she would stand ten toes down and smile through it. She reminded me what I should know by now: she likes to get her way. I rub a hand over my face, trying to push the sour memories back down, but they crawl up my throat anyway.

I know I gotta be honest with myself though: it wasn't just her. Deep down, I was afraid of being the "bad" guy and hurting her feelings by breaking things off and for once I wanted for once to be right. Our relationship wasn't always like that; it crept in disguised as care. Control took root. In her eyes, I was always wrong no matter how deluded the situation was. And as much as I tried, I could never be the man she needed, nor could I picture a future with her, no matter how hard I tried to convince myself otherwise.

I allowed this to continue until the ultimate straw: the day after my grandfather's funeral. I didn't send her a "good morning" text as I usually did, but apparently, the fact that I could barely get out of bed or check my phone wasn't a good enough excuse. She didn't care. As a man, I was always supposed to text her first thing in the morning, anything otherwise was proof that I just *had* to be cheating. But in the middle of her calling me and going off like usual—accusing me of being a selfish fuckboy and ignoring her—something in me broke. I said I was done and that I meant it this time. She balked at the time but swore up and down I'd come back. It was only after a couple weeks of silence that she began to realize I was serious, and in a move I now recognize as desperate and control-seeking, she reached out insisting we maintain a "friendship" and used that premise to stick around. But even though nothing romantic existed between us anymore (that part ended several months prior to the breakup anyway) the same cycle continued into our new dynamic, and I still found myself feeling nervous about that edge in her voice.

"You really saying I can't visit? We're supposed to be friends, Khalid."

My frustration grows and I rub my face to keep my voice calm.

"This isn't a friendship, Sharie. It never has been. And the fact that you've been acting like we're still together—"

"Oh, so you got somebody over there?" She cuts me off. "You moved on that fast, huh?"

*It's been three whole months, I think. My moving on wasn't fast, but long overdue.*

"No, I don't. But that's not the point. Even if I did, I don't owe you an explanation. We're not together anymore." Her eyes narrow.

"You ain't shit, Khalid." I sigh.

"Take care of yourself, Sharie. I mean that."

She hangs up, and I block her number right then and there before anything else happens. I drop my phone onto my chest, take a deep breath, and stare at the ceiling. It's only 7:15 a.m., but my heart is pounding—There's no way I'm falling back asleep now.

After a few more minutes of laying around restlessly, I swing my legs out of the bed and head to the kitchen. The fridge hums like it's thinking too hard. The contents inside of it: a bottle of water, burger king leftovers, and a protein shake. I stare at my "options" for a beat, shake my head, and let out a dry laugh.

*Yeah, it's time to be an adult and buy some groceries.*

I head to the bathroom to brush my teeth, rinse my face, and catch my reflection in the mirror. My eyes still look tired, but lighter—like something in me has finally unclenched. I throw on an old tee and a pair of shorts, grab my AirPods, and sling my gym bag over my shoulder. Minutes later, I'm on my motorcycle, a new calm settling in my chest as the breeze hits my skin. I can't explain it, but it makes me smile.

Before accepting my current contract, I made sure everything I needed would be close by. While six and half months is temporary, it's long enough for me to want convenience. Thankfully, the hospital where I'm working is less than fifteen minutes away from where I'm staying, and the grocery store, downtown, and the gym are within a short range too. Usually travel contracts aren't this long but with two of the staff on maternity leave, and one on sick leave, this was an exception. I knew it would be a huge change and adjustment but I believe that's exactly what I need, so I jumped at the opportunity when my recruiter told me.

When I arrive at my new gym, I feel a little excitement—like a 'lil ass kid at a playground. Working out has always been a part of my life since I was in high school. It's how I clear my mind and get myself right, both mentally and physically. I head straight to the first open bench to claim it, but just as I begin adjusting the weights, a flash of bright pink crosses my peripheral. I glance up. A girl with curly brown hair, dressed in a pink workout set that hugs every curve, walks toward the exit. *Goddamn, she's beautiful.* I catch myself staring, shake it off, and refocus on my lift, letting the adrenaline kick in. I turn up my music and push through the first set. As I'm working through it and nodding my head to Jeezy, my music cuts off abruptly, interrupted by a buzzing vibration in my pocket. I set my weights down and fish my phone out of my shorts, glancing down at the screen: *Mom.*

"Hey Ma," I say, wiping sweat from my brow.

"Son! I miss you. Did you forget your mom already?" Her voice carries a familiar calm, the kind that makes everything feel a little lighter. "How's my boy doing? How's work? Are you eating right? Sleeping okay?" I'm smiling before I even realize it.

"Hey, Ma. Never that, and I miss you, too. Work's not so bad. The first week was smooth, can't complain. I'm actually coming up on my first night shift when I go back after my days off."

"Well, I hope so, Khalid. I worry, you know I do. But I'm proud of you, baby. Proud you're stepping out, taking this contract, doing your thing."

"Thanks, Mom. That means a lot," I say. "And how's Dad doing?" I add. "Still glued to the same spot on the couch watching football?" I chuckle at my own joke, and so does she.

"Yup, pretty much. He hasn't moved since you left," she says.

I shake my head playfully.

"He got that Dallas Cowboys mug in his hand?"

"Sho' do," she replies. I can hear the smile in her voice.

"What are you doing now?" she asks.

"Oh, just getting a workout in, Ma. It's my first actual day off."

There's a pause on her end, just long enough that I notice the subtle shift in her tone. Then she exhales, and I catch it—something beneath the lightheartedness.

"Ahh, okay. Well, I won't keep you—just know mama misses you,

Khalid. Ever since your grandpa passed, it feels like...every day is so short. Life's short, son, and I just want to soak in every minute I can with you—but I know I also need to let you soak up your own fresh start and embrace it."

I nod, even though she can't see me. There's a weight in her words—a little sadness mixed in with love. She talks now as if life is so fleeting, as if every day counts double because she knows how fast it can all slip away. I've noticed her do that more and more since Grandpa passed. But she's right. I needed this today, I think. I need to allow myself to embrace this fresh start.

"Love you, Mama," I say softly.

"Love you, too, son. Be careful, okay? You're my firstborn, I can't have nothing happening to you."

"I will. I'll call you to check in again soon," I promise.

"Bye, son."

I hang up, slipping my phone back into my pocket. I take a deep breath, pick up my weights, and push into the next set.

After my workout and before heading back to my Airbnb, I swing by the grocery store with a brief list: eggs, ground beef, some veggies. I've never really spent time in the kitchen, so cooking for myself is going to be...interesting, to say the least. But I know I can't keep eating out every day, so I force myself into this unfamiliar territory and hope for the best.

Back at the Airbnb, the space is nothing special—it's a single-bed studio with a mounted TV, a standard bathroom, and a kitchen that's the size of a hallway. It's the kind of place that screams "three-star man cave," but I can make it work for now.

After stashing away my groceries, I make a protein shake, throw on a pair of headphones and start up a video game. The quiet presses in around me. There's no one to answer to, and no one else's expectations to meet. Instead, there's time to breathe and think—something I haven't had since Sharie entered my life. Once I feel sufficiently relaxed, I get up and whip up a quick meal. I plate my ground beef into five taco shells, topping it off with some diced tomatoes and avocado before taking my first bite. I let out a small smile as the flavors sink onto my tongue. Surprisingly, the food is pretty good. I fall back onto the couch, then, plate in one hand, controller in the other, letting everything blur together.

*

Wrapping up the charting for my last patient, I quickly type to complete the day's work. In just a few minutes, it'll be 7:00 a.m., and I'll finally be off the clock from work. Though I'm more adjusted to this hospital given that I'm going on my third week here, this night shift has me beat. As soon as I get to the Airbnb, I'm back to my routine: catch up on rest, gym, meal prep, and of course video games. Once I finish giving my report to Sierra, the RN who will be taking over my patients, I notice she's stalling and trying to chat about everything except the job.

"So, Khalid, how are you liking it here so far?" she asks, setting her clipboard down, eyeing me.

"It's good. Everyone's been welcoming. The weather's dope." She tilts her head, a playful smile curving her lips.

"Done any exploring yet or hung out with anyone from around here? It's been what—almost a month now? You're not hiding from us, are you?" I zip my bag, not bothering to correct her that I've been here just barely three weeks, though the time already feels like it's flying.

"Nah, I haven't really had the chance to go out since I've been so busy adjusting,no sightseeing, either," I reply. She leans closer, voice teasing.

"Well, we should change that. Let's get drinks. Or just...grab a bite and go somewhere fun? Give me your number and I'll text you." I sigh inwardly at the direction our conversation has taken, but her forwardness catches me off guard, so I hand her my phone anyway. She smirks, taps her number, then holds it out. Her fingers linger on mine just a beat too long. Something about her eagerness–the way she fills every pause–makes me uneasy. I've seen this version of interest

16

before, it's surface level and I've already learned how easily it stops feeling mutual.

"We should work out together too," she adds. "You're clearly serious about your fitness."

"Cool, cool," I say dryly, fishing for my keys and walking backward slowly, hoping she catches the hint. "Catch you later." I give a half-hearted wave and finally turn on my heel to leave.

"Bye, Khalid!" She sings after me.

I can't get on my bike fast enough. It's like I'm late getting home when I don't have shit going on but a nap and a workout.

*

Leaving the gym, sweat cooling on my skin, I wander down the street instead of heading back tomy Airbnb. The sun's out, and there's no humidity clinging to me like it does back home in Florida. As I'm walking, I notice a small shop on the corner called Charmed. The bold, artsy sign above it is what catches my eye initially, then the cookies lined up in the window display seal the deal. I push the door open—and freeze.

*Shit, it's her: the girl from the gym.*

Our eyes meet. Her smile hits me in the chest.

"Hi there! What can I get you started with?" she asks, voice warm. I stammer for a second, still too stunned to remember how to speak.

"Hey, what's up?" I say, trying to play it cool. "Lemme get a chocolate cookie?"

"Good choice," she responds approvingly. "I just baked them."

"You made these?" I ask, wanting to hear her voice again.

"Yeah, it's our own little recipe. I'm pretty proud of it," she says modestly.

"Well, now I'm really excited. What drink do you recommend

pairing it with? I'm not really much of a coffee guy, but I see y'all have tea too."

"Ooh, you put me on the spot! Well, since I was actually just making an iced banana matcha latte...Would you want one too?" I eye the muddy concoction in the blender under her hand, but something tells me to just go with it.

"Alright, I'll trust you. Looks like it tastes like the earth, though." She laughs and starts making my drink. I catch myself watching her as she moves behind the counter. She stands five feet tall, and her skin glows warm like golden caramel. Her lips are full and plush with a natural tint. I notice the curve of her legs, and the way her thick voluminous small curls flow around her face and down her back. She hands me a cup; I take a sip.

"Oh, this shit fire."

"Told you I wasn't lying!" she giggles. Got damn, she's stunning.

"Are you from Cali?" she asks.

"Nah. Florida."

"Really? What brings you out here?"

"I'm a travel nurse. Got here a few weeks ago." Her light brown eyes widen.

"I respect that! Being a nurse is a very intense job. Congrats on the contract. How's it going so far?"

"Good! The people here are cool. The weather's perfect. I don't sweat," I joke. She laughs into her matcha.

"What do you mean, you don't sweat?"

"Florida's humidity is different."

"Oh, true I know. Our mom used to live in Florida. Humidity is wild. My hair would blow up to the ceiling." I grin at the image she paints in my mind.

"Big hair looks good on you." It slips out before I can stop it. She glances down, a shy smile curling her lips.

"Thanks," she replies. I change the subject, then, not wanting to scare her off.

"You said you used to live in Florida?"

"Yeah, but then our mother passed away."

"Oh...I'm sorry."

"It's alright. Well—it's not. But...grief isn't linear, you know?"

*Don't I know it.*

"But I'm here with my sisters," she continues. "And I'm grateful for that. Actually, that's one of them over there—Destiny." She turns her attention to her sister, then, and calls out, "Hey, Dee! Say hi!"

"Hiii!" Destiny waves on command before returning her focus back to her work.

"You both work here?" I ask. She nods, proud.

"We own the shop." I raise an eyebrow.

"For real? That's amazing. This place is beautiful."

"Thank you. It's our little piece of home. And that matcha you're drinking is my signature special."

"Well, I'm honored," I say. "What do I owe you?" She stops me.

"On the house. Consider it a gift. Welcome to Cali."

"Oh, no, I can't do that." I laugh, pulling out a twenty. "Ask my family—I don't roll like that." She laughs, ready to argue.

"What's your name, anyway?" she cuts in, playful but curious.

"Khalid."

"Khalid..." She says it softly, like poetry. "I love that name."

"And yours?"

"Mia."

"It was a pleasure, Mia." I drop the twenty. "Thank you for the matcha. And the conversation."

"Anytime," she says warmly.

I don't want to stop talking to her, but I don't want to take up too much of her time, either. Taking my cup, I head toward the door, a softness spreading through me. She offers a final smile and turns her back to me to wrap an arrangement. The bell above the door hinge chimes, announcing my exit as I walk out. After a few steps, I stop to indulge in the cookie she baked. I let out a soft groan; this is delicious.

Chocolate chips in every bite.

Yeah—I'm coming back here.

# CHAPTER THREE
## *Mia*

The bell rattles softly behind Khalid as he leaves the shop. I pause in the middle of wrapping an arrangement, stealing one last glance at the door before it swings shut. Did that just happen? I watch him as the sun carves out his broad shoulders and back. Tattoos trail down his warm brown skin like secrets he kept, but doesn't bother to hide. Even with all that muscle, there's a gentleness about him. He was so easy to talk to. Part of me wishes he'd stayed just a little longer. I shake my head to erase the thought from my mind and bounce back to fixing the arrangement. *Let me stop. That man is six foot FOINE, bearded, and fit with the kind of build that takes space without trying. He's clearly spoken for.* Just then, Destiny appears out of nowhere, practically vibrating with nosy excitement.

"Sooooo...who was that?" She's cheesing from ear to ear, damn near dancing in place, ready for the tea. I play it cool, wrapping the ribbon around the bouquet.

"Just a customer. His name's Khalid. He came in to check out the shop." Destiny gasps dramatically.

"Is he from here? Did you get his number? Y'all were talking forever." I roll my eyes, fighting a smile.

"Nope. Didn't get his number. And he's not from here—he's from Florida. He's just on a nursing contract. But who knows? Maybe I'll run into him again." She squints at me, unconvinced.

"Mmmhm. Okay, anyway, chop chop—we gotta finish up. Prue's landing soon, and our sister night is calling."

"Yes, ma'am." I say setting the finished arrangement aside. "Let's wrap up."

José clocks out for his shift. Together, Destiny and I knock out the last of the tea orders and clean up the counters. With everything neat and stocked, we grab our bags and head home, ready for our sister night.

*

"HELLO, HELLO! I HAVE RETURNED—IT IS I! Come and gather, witches!" Prue bursts through the front door like she is the moment, and let's be clear—Prue is that girl. With her jet black mermaid wavy curls that spill down her back, thick eyebrows and dark brown eyes, her features sit against her warm golden tone complexion. Her face rarely portrays amusement, and naturally carries an unbothered expression. Her smile is something you need to earn. We joke that she's our Maleficent, all quiet authority and stillness.

I laugh from my room, shutting my laptop with a little clap and make my way to meet her at the door.

"SHE HATH RETURNED AND GRACED US WITH HER PRESENCE!" I yell back, half-joking, half-serious. Destiny pops her head out from her room, equally dramatic.

"YES! SHE HATH RETURNED—LET US CELEBRATE!" We all meet at the front door in a rush of giggles and squeals, arms flung around each other in a three-way hug that makes me feel fourteen again for a second.

"Okay, okay, get off me!" Prue complains, but she's laughing, so Destiny and I just squeeze her tighter.

Prue's never been the affectionate type. Life's circumstances made her grow up fast. Before Mom passed, all of us lived crammed together in a tiny one-bedroom apartment. Mom was terrible with money and worse with boundaries. Prue carried the weight of that recklessness young. She made sure we had food and kept the lights on when Mom didn't. She shielded us from the mess as best she could.

Our mother's obsession with religion was unhealthy. Sure, there were times where she wasn't being the best version of herself and even hurtful in many moments, but I also attribute some of that behavior to the quiet indoctrination of the churches—how they blurred the lines of faith and fear, and guilt and obedience, particularly when it came to paying tithes. Gone our money went and landlords plastered eviction notices on our door like Pizza Hut coupons. While our mom might have found solace in prayer, Prue saw it as a dangerous illusion, an awful attempt to shield us from the harsh realities of life.

When I was fifteen years old, Prue moved out and I started working as a busser at a restaurant. From the moment I started working, my clothes, bus fare, food at school, and phone bill became my responsibility. Needing money for food, I shamefully called my father—"Dad, could you send me $20? I'm hungry and have no money"—and he would always respond with an annoyed tone in his voice. "Aren't you working? What did you do with your money?" Embarrassment would come over me as I spoke, my voice barely a whisper. "I paid my phone bill and bought some sneakers for school." My voice trailed off, my words feeling hollow and inadequate. His response was swift and sharp, a cutting blade aimed at my already fragile self-esteem. "Well, that's your fault," he'd said in a stern tone. "You shouldn't have spent money on shoes!" His words suffocated any remaining hope of understanding or support.

Years later, we talked about those harsh exchanges, and even though time has passed, he was still just as defensive as before. He said we had no right to be upset that he didn't send us money for food. He said we should blame our mom for not using the child support he gave more wisely—even though it was only $300 a month. Prue pushed back, but he often doubled down, turning our struggles into something we should be ashamed of. It stung. Somehow, we were supposed to carry the weight of our mom's mistakes—mistakes that he, too, dealt with in his own time with her.

Prue stepped in when this originally happened. She sent us food. She was only twenty-four at the time. Our big sister, our best friend— and in a lot of ways, a second mother to us. She's always been that way. Strong, grounded. She doesn't let just anyone in, but when she loves, it's real. Her presence carries weight. She doesn't need to say much—her confidence speaks through her silence. She gives off a quiet intensity. As we got older, our father despised this. He saw it as her being a rebel and disrespectful, labeling her defiant and demanding she conform. The truth, however, laid much deeper. His attempts to control her stemmed from his inability to accept her. He deliberately misconstrued her, painting her in a negative light, a maneuver facilitated by his wife's dislike for Prue. He mocked her for her apartment and weaponized his material possessions, hoping to diminish her by saying her son is at her mercy to succeed. But she never let it break her.

What my father could never understand is that Prue knew who she was and could not be molded. Now, she and her son live together by the water, fulfilling her lifelong dream. She's a flight attendant with a small business on the side, she's a reiki healer and she also supports women and their maternity journeys.

"So, what should we start with? Tarot? Deep talks about our childhood with an episode rerun of *Charm*?" Destiny asks eagerly with excitement.

"Yes to all that!" I answer while turning my back to fetch a bottle of wine. Destiny reaches for her tarot deck while Prue pours our wine glasses and puts together our snack spread. "So, Prue, how was your date?" I ask as I join her in preparing snacks.

"It was really nice. The restaurant was pleasant, so we went for coffee afterward." Her smile grows as she recounts the details. "Before we said goodbye at the airport, we kissed," she adds with a smirk.

"Awwww, Prue, you like him." Destiny says playfully, teasingly.

Prue sucks her teeth and waves her hand at our silliness. "Antouka…" she says in Haitian creole. "We will see where it goes with time and if he continues to act right," she retorts.

The three of us hang out and talk for hours. Prue is only in town for a day before she takes off for work again, so we soak up every minute. We repeat the same inside jokes that even years later haven't lost their charm. We retell the same childhood stories we know by heart, each memory unfolding like a special photo album. While reminiscing, our hands move through the tarot deck, drawing cards and interpreting them in between sips of wine and bites of our favorite snacks. The night ends with familiar nostalgia and the unbreakable bond of sisterhood.

*

Today is my Pilates day. Even though it's been a while, I still stick to level 1.5, but I think at this point, I know Pole dancing is way more my vibe—that's where it's at for me. I keep telling myself I'll get back to it soon. As class wraps up, I step out into the open gym just in time for a familiar silhouette to catch my eye. My heart jumps a little. It's him. Time stops for a beat. Then he spots me and calls me out, looking entirely too pleased with himself.

"Yoo!"

Khalid strides over, every step making it impossible not to notice the curve of his biceps, the tank top stretched across his chest that's doing absolutely nothing. His eyes smile with his mouth.

That's already my favorite part—warm, easy, inviting.

"Hi, Khalid. You stalking me?" I tease.

"I could ask you the same thing," he shoots back, wrapping one arm around me for a hug that lingers just a little. "You come here often?" He pulls back, playful.

"Yes, we actually own this gym." He pauses and looks at me as his eyes grow wide.

"Ha, that's a good joke ain't it!? I'm fuckin with you," I say, still cracking up. He laughs.

"Okay, you funny; you got jokes."

"You signed up here too?"

"Month-to-month. I'm only here for roughly six months, so no point in anything long-term."

"I see." I respond nonchalantly.

"What have you got planned today? Are you off and a free gyal?" he asks, slipping a hint of a Caribbean accent into the end just to make me laugh—and it works.

"I am indeed a free gal. I just need to grab some stuff from the farmers' market. Then maybe hit the beach to write for a bit. What about you?"

"Other than the gym? Nothing. This area's still new to me." I bite my lip for half a second before it slips out:

"Wanna check out the beach with me?"

*Ew, why do I sound like I'm asking him on a date?*

"Yeah. I've never been to a beach here on the West Coast. Let me get your number. We'll meet at your shop?" I keep my cool as I hand over my phone.

"Sure." He types it in, sends himself a text.

"Alright. I'll see you in a bit."

I nod, turning away trying to play it off, but my smile is doing the most.

*

I push the door open with my hip, groceries bag straps digging into my palms from the weight.

"Destiny, I'm home!" She glances up from the couch, phone in hand.

"Hey suga, you took forever." I set the bags on the counter and lean back on the kitchen island, my mouth tugging at the corners.

"Guess who I saw?" Her eyes lift, curious.

"Who?"

"That fine ass man from the shop." Destiny sits up straighter.

"You're lying."

"I'm not," I say, trying and failing to hide my smile. "We ran into each other at the gym." She squints at me with a teasing smile.

"How convenient."

"Shut uppp," I groan. I start unpacking groceries, setting fruit on the counter. "Anyway...we're actually linking up in a little bit. He wants to see the beach." Destiny's mouth gapes at me.

"MIA." I shake my head, attempting to escape her gaze and move to the stove, grabbing the kettle.

"Relax! You want tea? I'm making some."

"Yes," she says instantly, sliding off the couch, coming closer to the kitchen island. As the kettle fills, she leans on the counter beside me, eyes sparkling.

"Soo you're seeing him again? Today?" I shrug, trying to keep it cool as I reach for my mug.

"Yeah, I'm going to get ready in a couple minutes."

"Oh, this is a *date*." Destiny says with a sly smile like she's seen my future.

"It's not a date," I protest.

"Mia's got a DATE," she sings, wagging her phone at me. I roll my eyes so hard they might stick.

"It's not. He's just new here. I'm being nice."

"Mmhmm. Be nice then. Not too nice though—the ocean don't need to see ass and titties in the daytime!" She shoots me a smirk.

"HA! GIRL BYE!" I say, flipping her off with a grin as I head to my bathroom to get ready. I peek at my phone as soon as the door closes behind me.

*Khalid: I should be there soon. Hope you're not scared of bikes.*

Bikes? I glance at my reflection.

*My workout fit is not about to cut it.*

But I don't want to look like I'm doing the most either. Beach casual. That's the move. I swap into my white ribbed strapless bikini top and my flowy brown maxi skirt. If he really has a bike, well...we'll figure it out. I fluff my curls, put on my gold hoops, add a touch of gloss over my brown lip liner, and grab my crossbody to head to my car.

*

The ride over feels longer than it is. When the shop comes into view, so does he. I catch myself staring. There he is—standing next to a motorcycle, helmet in hand, smile big enough to knock the wind out of me. He's changed, too—fresh tank, basketball shorts, fitted cap on. Brown skin glistening in the sun and his gold grill flashes me when he smiles at me.

*Why are you so fine?*

"What's good, Mia?" He says, cheesing at me.

"Heyyy." I eye the bike warily. "So you weren't kidding." He taps the rose decal on the helmet he picks up.

"Got you one, too. You ready?" I lift my skirt slightly, my crooked smile giving me away.

"You sure you can handle both of us on your bike?" I ask and he laughs simultaneously.

"Na, but you brave for trusting me though. Come on!" I slip the helmet on, lift my skirt, and swing my leg over, arms sliding around his waist like it was the perfect fit.

"Hold on tight," he says, voice muffled by his helmet.

*Don't mind if I do.*

The engine roars, and we peel off into the streets, the wind pulling my squeals straight from my chest and burying them against his back. I feel like I'm in a movie. It only just occurred to me that I've never ridden on the back of a motorcycle before.

"Damn," he says, pulling off his helmet just as we arrive at El Matador Beach, eyes scanning the sea caves like a kid seeing magic for the first time. "This is beautiful. Seen nothing like it." I tug mine off, too, curls tumbling loose.

"I come here all the time. It's my place. I read, write...sometimes just sit and let the ocean tell me my business." He laughs as he takes a look over the edge to see the stairs leading down to the beach.

"Got damn, I didn't realize we were doing cardio this afternoon?"

"HA! It's my thank-you for the bike ride. Now come on! We're climbing down." We begin making our way carefully down the steps.

"So, what's your family background?" he asks.

"My mom's side is Haitian," I say, glancing over at him. "She was born in Port-au-Prince and came to the States when she was in her late twenties. Most of her family's still back in Haiti in a town called Arcahaie. Her dad was part Middle Eastern, and everyone else is Haitian. My dad was born in New York but now lives here in Cali—He's Black American." I smile. "What about you?"

"Looks like we both got Caribbean in us. My mom's family was born and raised in Jamaica, my father's side Black American."

"Oh, wow! That's so dope, I wasn't expecting that. Being Caribbean is a different kind of flex."

"It really is, our household carries itself in such a unique way that only we understand," he says proudly.

"If that ain't the truth, I love it so deeply!"

"And don't get me started on Carnival," he adds. "The colors, the music—it's dope!"

I laugh. "And is!! Oh my gosh I've always wanted to put on those beautiful costumes. They're so elaborate, it's still on my bucket list. Have you been to J'Ouvert?"

"Hellll yeah I've been to J'Ouvert, went three years in a row with my boys."

"J'Ouvert goes crazy forreal, it's so much fun. I would spend days washing the paint out of my hair but it's worth it."

"Oh I bet, and you got a lot of hair too."

I laugh. "Anyway, how are you liking the hospital you're contracted at?" I ask as we continue down the steps.

"I like it, it's alright," he replies, though his tone carries a hint of uncertainty, as if he's not even sure of his own answer.

"Something wrong?"

"No, nothing's wrong. I actually enjoy my time here. It's just...the hospital is just that—the hospital and my workplace. After several years, it feels like the same work, just different hospital beds and rooms. Emotional detachment helps me cope with how intense work can be. I enjoy my job, I take it very seriously, but it gets heavy. I work with all kinds of patients, occasionally I float between departments, but most of the time I'm in the NICU and PICU."

"Oh my goodness, with the little ones?"

"Yeah, they pull on my heartstrings all the time." I nod.

"I can imagine," I say, letting his words settle before continuing. "Can I ask why you chose California? I mean, it's so far from your home. Do you miss it?" He exhales deeply, as though releasing a weight he's been carrying. His gaze drifts for a moment before returning with quiet resolve.

"I came here for a fresh start. My grandfather, who I was really close to, passed away a few months ago."

"Oh, Khalid, I'm so sorry."

"Thank you. I don't think I fully allowed myself to grieve for him. I feel like if I do, then it's real." He pauses. "Around the time we buried him, I went through a breakup. While it was necessary and my call, it all felt like a ton of bricks weighing on my shoulders. I've always stuck to what I knew; I went to community college and nursing school locally. It all felt safe. So this temporary move feels big, I never saw myself leaving Florida." He exhales again, this time lighter, less burdened. "I'm glad I did it. I think my grandpa would've wanted this for me. My mom struggled with me leaving at first, but still supported me." He pauses again, then shifts the conversation.

"Anyway...were you born and raised in Cali?"

"You should be proud. A big jump across the country is no small feat. Also...Thank you for sharing about your grandfather." A beat passes. "And to answer your question, yes, I was born here. My sisters and I grew up in the city."

"The city?" he repeats, unsure if he heard me right.

"Yeah, San Francisco" I say, knowingly. "We left maybe two years ago, we got our business here in SoCal, and got pretty planted here."

"Was it always your goal to open a cafe-flower shop?"

"Not always. Actually, my sister worked at a lab, and I worked at a university in Northern California. Combining our favorite things— coffee, tea, and flowers, we took a chance. Since then, it's been really successful. It was demanding in the beginning, but we've found our balance. Hired staff to help. Overall, our success makes us feel truly blessed. At some point I would like to add a bookshelf featuring Indie authors."

"The shop really is beautiful. I'm glad I walked in that day and that's a great idea, it would match the aesthetic of it easily."

"Thank you." I pause before continuing. "Khalid, I know I just met you, but I feel your grandfather would be so proud of you. I hope I'm not overstepping." He stops and glares at me.

"You're not, he meant a lot to me. He was, and remains, really important to me. When I get back to Florida I plan to visit his grave and...talk to him." His voice trails off.

There's a brief pause as a little kid nearby kicks a ball in our direction, giggling as it rolls past. Khalid scoops it up and tosses it back to the boy. I notice the kid's parents watching not far in the distance, smiling at their child's antics. "What a cutie pie," I murmur.

"You see yourself having kids?" he asks.

"Yeah...someday. But I'm in no rush." I glance down at my hands, thinking of the shop and how recently our business has really taken off. "Right now, I'm pretty content where I am. But someday...I want a chunky baby."

"Chunky, huh?"

"Yes, chunky, what about you?" The kid runs back to his parents, taking his ball with him. Khalid's eyes light up, a little smile tugging at his lips.

"I do. I got a little niece back home and she's a ray of sunshine. I really love kids, and I think I'd be a great dad. I want a baby girl someday." He takes a pause.

"You know after I met you at your shop I didn't think I'd see you again." I'm blushing a bit. I just know it.

"I didn't think we'd run into each other again either let alone this quick, but this town has a way of circling folks back around. It's a good thing we did, I mean who else is gonna show you around SoCal? I'm like your only friend." I joke as I start walking ahead of him.

"You got jokes," he teases while smirking. "All that excitement sounds like you ain't got any friends, either." he says playfully.

I laugh, and before I can come up with a clever comeback, he casually lays his arm around my shoulders, pulling me closer as we walk. His touch is warm, effortless, like it belongs there.

Before we make our way back up the stairs to his bike, we exchange Instagram handles and carry on with more conversation, the lightness of it all settling over us like a comfortable blanket. Khalid hands me the rose decal helmet he picked up for me prior to linking up. I climb on behind him, aware of the closeness right away. His shoulders, broad, back solid; I feel his muscles shifting under this thin tank when he leans forward. I hold the back of his traps instead of his waistline this time as we merge onto the freeway. Not even to steady myself, but because I want to feel him. The sky is doing its romantic thing—soft pinks deepening blue in the horizon. On one side of the freeway, the ocean stretches out alongside us, the wind carries salt off the water. This afternoon was so simple yet so different in contrast from my last outing with a man. Causal but still this just feels...*right.*

Khalid cuts off the engine, and the silence settles in easy. He pulls off his helmet and glances over at me.

"Aye, thanks for showing me around today," he says. "I needed that." I unbuckle my helmet and shake out my curls; I just know they're slightly pressed on the back side.

"The beach—especially that one—is always a vibe. You're welcome." I say handing back the helmet he got for me. He steps off the bike, offers his hand without a word, and helps me down like it's second nature. We don't rush toward my car. The walk is slow, quiet, like both of them are trying not to disrupt whatever's lingering in the air.

"You ever take people there?" he teases, shooting me a look. I smirk.

"You're the first." He raises his eyebrows.

"Oh? Say less. I'm VIP now!"

"Listen! don't do too much!" I laugh. We reach my car and turn to face each other, leaning lightly against the door. He maintains a respectful distance, surveying me.

"I wanna see you again," he confesses. I nod my head at him.

"Okay...sure." I hesitate for a split second and I'm not sure if he catches it.

Do I wanna see him again? *Hell yeah.* But is it a good idea?.... I swallow the thought to avoid answering it. Six months is six months.

*I best make it worth my while.*

"What you got going on Saturday?" he asks, still close to me but very gentle.

"I'm free in the evening, let's say around five?"

"Okay, let me take you to dinner."

"I'd like that," I reply, unlocking my door. He walks back to his bike, glancing over his shoulder once.

"Drive safe, Mia."

"You too, Khalid."

I slide into my seat, close the door, and take a breath before even turning the key. My reflection in the rearview shows it plain—that subtle, involuntary smile.

# CHAPTER FOUR
## *Khalid*

I finish adjusting the IV line, making sure the drip rate is steady before I tape it down. My elderly patient lets out a slow breath, the meds finally easing into his system. His wife sits on the other side of the bed, their fingers laced together. She's been here every single day for the last three weeks since he was brought in.

"Thank you, Khalid," she says with relief threaded in her voice—the kind people only use when their fear finally has somewhere to rest. "He hasn't looked this comfortable all day."

"He's doing well. I'll keep checking on him but just hit the call button if anything feels off." She nods gratefully.

"We appreciate you."

I'm not great at lingering in moments like that, so I just nod again and slip out of the room, letting the door close behind me. Out in the hall, I log into the computer station and start charting—vitals, response to treatment, next steps. My hands move on autopilot, but my mind's somewhere else completely. Truly, I wanna see Mia again. I glance at my phone and begin texting her.

*Me: Hey Mia, how's your day going?*

I make my way into the hallway to head toward the break room.

"Khalidddd! What are you doing after work?"

I put my phone down. Without turning around, I know exactly who is singing my name. I feel a tap on my shoulder. I turn to see Sierra grinning at me.

"What's up, Sierra?"

"What are your plans?" she asks, her tone playful but expectant.

"I was gonna work out—"

"Nope! Not anymore. You're coming to the bar with us!" she cuts me off before I can finish.

"Oh, I don't know…I'm pretty tired." I respond, hoping she'll take the hint.

"Oh, come on, Khalid! You need to hang out. I'm not taking no for an answer."

It's just one night. How bad could it be with other people around? And besides, maybe this will help me avoid the one-on-one hangout she keeps insisting on…

"Alright, I'll go."

"YES!" She claps her hands together, full of excitement. "Meet us on Harbor Blvd. There are food trucks and tables right outside the bar—it's basically our spot."

"Okay, sounds good." I reply dryly. As she walks off, I grab my backpack and check my phone, hoping to see a reply from Mia.

*Mia: Hi Khalid, it's really busy at the shop, but that's not a bad thing. So, I'd say my day is going pretty well. How's your day?*

*Me: I'm happy your day is going well. My day has been long but good. My coworkers want to hang out after work. I think I'll go. I've been saying no for a while because I want to relax.*

*Mia: I totally get wanting to chill in a comfy bed after a long day of work. But you can unwind socially too! Let me know how it goes.*

I start walking to my motorcycle, staring at my phone in my hand trying to figure out what to say next.

*Me: I'm looking forward to seeing you again. What are you in the mood for? Tell me and I'll find a nice restaurant.*

I pause next to the bike, thumb hovering over the screen.

*Mia: Likewise Khalid. And I like sushi.*

I sit on the bike seat, not even turning the engine on yet, just smiling at my screen like a fool.

*Me: Cool, I'll find a spot*

*Mia: A man doing the planning? Dangerous. I could get used to that.*

*Me: You can, I don't mind.*

I exhale a laugh as I put my helmet on and start the engine, the vibration of the bike matching the energy running through me. Friday can't come fast enough.

*

"Cheers to the new guy!" One of my coworkers calls out while raising his cocktail.

"Thank you, I'm not big on all the attention, but I appreciate you all being so welcoming," I reply, humbly.

Our glasses clink in the center of the group. Some hold their drinks high, while others instinctively reach for their phones, eager to capture the moment for social media.

"Khalid!" Sierra's voice cuts through the chatter, drawing my attention. "Let's take a pic."

"Uh...okay." She lays her arm on my shoulder and brings her head near mine and strikes the familiar duck-face pose. She then hands me her phone a moment later.

"Type in your IG," she demands. I hesitate, then slowly type in my username.

"It's about time we traded socials," she adds, flashing a satisfied smile.

I don't respond, instead I take a sip of my mule. The group continues to rally, getting rounds of drinks with meals from different trucks. Before too long, the chef from one of the food trucks yells out my order, so I stroll over to grab it and return with my tacos and a basket of chips with salsa.

"Khalid, what'd you get?" Sierra asks, already drifting into my space.

"Tacos and chips," I reply. She steals a chip before I'm even done talking.

"Okay, big muscles and carbs? Didn't think you'd risk the salsa dip." I chuckle. "The salsa dip."

She laughs and dips the chip again like it's hers. "Yeah! You're eating like you're trying not to mess up your shirt. Real focused. Like this taco owes you money."

"...Alright," I interrupt, deadpan. She cracks up.

"I'm just messing with you! I talk shit for fun!"

"Oh, I talk shit, too, trust me—I'm just enjoying my meal right now." I add a small smile to soften my words. She watches me, waiting for more, but I go right back to my taco. Trying again, she leans in.

"So...Do you plan on dancing tonight? The DJ always plays all the good hits when the crowd gets going."

I open my mouth to answer, but before I do, James, thankfully, inserts himself into our conversation.

"Yo, Khalid, we should hit the gym together!" He exclaims, his voice brimming with excitement.

"Yes, we should!" Sierra cuts back in almost immediately to include herself.

*Man, she really doesn't quit...How do I casually mention I'm seeing someone?*

Granted, I don't know that I can even call it that given my time is temporary here. Either way, fling or not, I can't stop thinking about her.

"Alright cool James, I'm down. Right now I'm at West fitness. They have trial passes and month-to-month terms you can do." I say as I take another sip of my drink.

"Alright, bet. I'll get your number before we go tonight."

Sierra's still watching me, intently waiting to hear what I'll say next. I glance at my phone, Mia's name sitting quietly in my text messages like a bookmark I keep returning to.

"Cool," I say to James. "I'll send you the gym address."

He gives me a thumbs-up. The night goes on with laughter and music. Some start dancing. But my head's already somewhere else.

## CHAPTER FIVE
### *Mia*

I wipe grip product off my palms when Chelsea claps for me, grinning like I just pulled off a miracle.

"Okay, Miaaa! That Superman was clean! And the butterfly? You locked it in." She gives me a proud nod, and something blooms in my chest. I laugh as I start packing up my gym bag.

"I was fighting for my life on that pole."

"And you won," she says, tossing me a towel. "You're getting stronger."

"I appreciate you,Chelsea, I could not do it without you as my instructor. Also, I'm trying to be more consistent," I say, stuffing my kneepads into the bag. My thighs are already blooming with small bruises, but honestly? Light work compared to usual. Chelsea leans against the pole, sipping from her water bottle.

"You know...if you ever feel like it, you should come to one of my choreo classes. No pressure. Bring your pleasers if you do, though." I raise an eyebrow.

"You think I'm ready for choreography?" She shrugs like it's obvious.

"Yes—and I think you'd have fun!"

"Ahhh...okay," I say, trying to play it cool. "I'll look into it."

"No pressure," she repeats. "Sounds good, love. Go home, take a hot bath, and stretch. Your body's gonna yell at you tomorrow. Love you!" I laugh.

"Love ya, girl! I respond. I sling my bag over my shoulder, and head for the door—still buzzing from nailing those moves. By the time I get home, all I want is a hot shower. I drop my gym bag by the floor of my room, peel off my clothes, walk into the shower and let the steam do its magic.

I begin prepping for my date with Khalid tonight, leaning over my bathroom sink with a beauty blender in one hand, and my phone balanced on the counter blasting old school R&B to keep my nerves from bouncing off the walls. Next to me, Destiny sits perched on the toilet lid like my personal hype-woman. She's been watching me do my makeup and hair for the last forty minutes.

"So this is, like, official-official?" she asks, clearly amused at my reflection. I roll my eyes but can't hide my smile.

"Yes. Official first date. Happy?"

"Extremely. He better feed you good, too—and don't you be shy with the menu either."

"True," I laugh, dabbing concealer under my eyes. "Honestly, I'm kinda excited."

"Good! Let yourself enjoy this. And if for any reason it's awkward, text me and I'll call with a fake emergency. Code word: greasy."

"Bye, Destiny." I flick water at her and she squeals, fleeing down the hall.

Alone again, I pause, staring at myself. First actual date in a minute. Deep breath. This is just a fling, it's time for some fun with someone who makes you laugh. I take one last look at myself in the mirror—hair big and curls soft, edges laid, a swipe of gloss over my brown lip liner and take another look at outfit. My black maxi halter top crochet dress hugs my curves in all the right places. Just then my phone lights up on the counter: a FaceTime call from Sage. I smile and slide to answer it.

"Hayyyy girllll!" She stops to gasp. "Where are we going, looking so good, sis?!" I set the phone down so it's propped so she can see my whole outfit and do a fun little twirl. "Yesssss, sis, and body TEA! That dress eats down!!" she says, continuing to hype me up.

"Thank you, sis! I have a lil' casual date tonight—nothing major," I say cheekily.

"A date?! Okay! You say 'casual,' but I still can't wait to hear about it...WHEN I SEE YOU!!" I grab the phone in excitement.

"Are the tickets booked officially? Are you flying in?"

"Yes, boo! I will be seeing you this weekend!" I let out a scream.

"Sage, this just made my whole day! I am so excited!"

"Me too, sis! We have so much to catch up on!" she says, beaming at the phone. "But I know you have a date, so I won't keep you on the phone. Have fun tonight, sis! I love you!" I crack up.

"Girl, you know me, cause I will talk all night and start up a whole new conversation right after saying bye," I say cheesing at her. "I love you so much, sis!" I add.

"Oh girl I know, I love you! I'll see you soon!"

We hang up and I check my inbox to find a new text awaiting me from not even three minutes ago:

*Khalid: Outside. If you got me waiting out here too long, I'm leaving you for the sushi chef.*

*Jk. Take your time, beautiful*

I bite my lip, trying and failing to hide the grin spreading across my face. From down the hall, Destiny's voice comes flying.

"Is that him? Mia! Is that him?!"

"Yes!" I yell back, grabbing my purse. She pops her head around the corner, squealing like a kid.

"Okay, okay, let's review: be cute, be safe, don't let him play with you, and text me the code word if you need me—"

"'Greasy,' I know!" I laugh, nudging past her. I step outside and there he is—standing next to his bike in the driveway, helmet resting on his knee, grin lazy and easy like he already owns the night. I pull out my phone and pretend to check something as I walk toward him, as if I'm not fully aware of him already.

"Hey, pretty girl," he calls, voice dipping low on purpose. I try to play it cool, but the way he looks at me knocks every plan right out of my head.

"Hi, Florida." He taps the helmet against his palm.

"About time. Lucky for you, you're worth the wait." He says playfully.

"Mmhm," I tease, taking the helmet. "Keep talking shit." He laughs.

"I'm playing, I know better than to rush a woman."

"Mama raised a gentleman, didn't she?" I say smiling as he leans in to hug me.

"She taught me a thing or two."

I put on my helmet—the same one he got me from last time with the rose on the side—and hop onto the bike behind him. We pull out and my arms lock tight around his waist. By the time we get to the sushi spot, my nerves are gone—replaced by that stupid grin he pulls out of me every five minutes.

*

We get inside the restaurant and waste no time playing awkward and cute, we order like we haven't eaten all day. Eventually we are down to one sushi roll and we both eye it like it just offended our families.

"Go 'head and take it," he says, leaning back like he's being generous. I squint.

"Nah, you take it. I already had the spicy tuna. I'm being fair."

"Fair?" He grabs his chopsticks dramatically.

"Nah, I'm a gentleman—plus, I'm not giving you anything to run back and tell your sisters." My hand flies to cover my mouth; I'm laughing so hard I nearly snort. He laughs, too, then cuts the roll like he's performing surgery. I reach over and slice it again, petty. We're giggling like kids. He pops a sad little piece in his mouth not larger than a dime, shakes his head.

"Damn. I'm full," he lies, pretending to struggle. "I can't eat another bite." We burst into another round of laughter. When it finally settles, I catch him watching me.

"What?" I say with a playful smile. He shrugs, voice softer now.

"Nothing. Just...glad I'm here with you."

I look down, pick up my napkin and reply, "Same." He pays the bill.

After dinner, we wander to the waterfront nearby. It's quiet, the air cooling down just enough that I press closer to him when the wind sneaks up. He walks slowly, matching my steps.

"I know you mentioned your mom before, but...is your dad around?" I shrug.

"He is. We're just...not super close."

"Why's that, if you don't mind my asking?"

"It's kind of lot and just messy.." He meets my gaze with an unguarded smile.

"I've got time."

"It's complicated, we used to be close but over time, things changed... He's not a bad man, just one of my deepest heartbreaks. Someone I love easier at a distance." I glance ahead as we walk. "We still talk, but it's brief. He has stepdaughters and we have some nice memories—partying, singing karaoke, things we've done for each other...But too often, it's like the calm never lasts long. I've just accepted that it probably never will." I pause, realizing how complex this sounds. "Sorry. I'm not doing a good job explaining this, am I?" He shakes his head gently.

"No, you are, I get it. I can tell your sisters mean everything to you, though. Sibling bonds are top tier. Do you think things with your dad could ever be different?"

"So true, my mantra is literally *Drink water and call your sisters*." I pause and chuckle. "Regarding my father, I don't know." I admit. "I asked for space because the drama got to be too much and petty at one point."

"That's big of you, stepping away rather than being reactive," he says. I exhale, the memory still sour.

"I agree, but instead of respecting it, my stepsister told everyone I was jealous of her relationship with my dad." I chuckle, the joy lost in that reminder and pain sunk in.

Khalid chuckles. "That's s uch a strange thing to say about y'all's father, like we are not just talking about some man. How old is she?"

"I want to say thir." His eyebrows shoot up.

"I would've thought you were talking about someone way younger, given the maturity level. That says more about her than it ever could about you."

"Yeah, I know it sounds crazier when I say it out loud." I laugh for real this time.

"So you're expected to keep the peace anyway?"

"Yeah, I'm cordial, that's it. I pray for my dad. As for that stepsister, I was never jealous of her. If anything, I was grieving the version of a father I always hoped would show up, since we used to be so close." Khalid is quiet for a moment before speaking.

"I can see that. I can also see how that was used against you." I nod.

"Yeah, I don't try to force it anymore, I just focus on me and my sisters. That's where my peace is.."

"I hear you," he says. "You shouldn't have to explain why you're choosing peace, people shouldn't put us in that position to begin with." I feel something loosen in my chest.

"It's big of you to still choose to pray for someone who hurt you. But also, I know how exhausting being the bigger person can be." *Damn he just gets it*, I think to myself. I want to kiss this man right now. And before I can stop myself—my lips clock in for work and are on his. I stopped to glance at him, realizing what I had done. There's a split second of a pause. I take a small step back. His eyes squint as a smile spreads across his face.

"Alright, come back here." he says, voice low and smooth. His arm wraps around me, fingers curling at my waist as he deepens the kiss, as if he's been waiting to kiss me all night. The heat between us is undeniable, like something we both knew was coming, but never quite expected to happen like this. And just like that, I know I'm in trouble.

"Yeah. I wasn't planning on that."

"Well," he says, voice low, "if that was unplanned, I can't wait to see what you do on purpose." I smile, shaking my head as I lean back a little to look at him.

"You always like this?"

"Like what?"

"Calm. Easy to be around. Funny without trying." He shrugs.

"Nah. Just with you."

"Is that right?" I chuckle. "Well, thank you," I say, quieter now.

"For what?"

"For holding space. For not trying to fix it, just...listening." I glance at the time and sigh then look at my watch to check the time.

"Damn, time already? You just gonna kiss me and leave?" he says, pulling me in to hold me. I groan.

"Ugh, I want to hang out longer, but I have to open the shop tomorrow. It's gonna be a busy morning—I've got tea orders to ship out." He puts a hand to his chest, dramatic.

"Okay. Let me let you focus before I end up calling you outta your job."

"Khalid, shut up!" I'm cracking up as we head back toward his bike. We arrive back at my place and he walks me to my door.

"What do you have planned for this weekend?" He asks.

"One of my girlfriends is actually in town from Florida and is stopping by my shop, we're going to catch up."

"I hope you both have a nice time." There's a moment of silence. He places his hand on the back of my neck and pulls me in for a gentle kiss.

"Thank you for letting me take you out tonight, I haven't laughed like that in a while."

"Of course, Khalid and I appreciated it too. You're so warm."

"I'll see you again soon," he says.

"Sounds good, have a great night, Khalid." I say as I turn my back to unlock my door.

"You, too, sweetheart."

*

I finish wrapping up a jar of honey and a couple of loose-leaf tea packs in a brown paper bag for

the customer in front of me.

"Thank you for coming," I say as I hand it over.

"Oh, of course! It's so nice to see how much your shop has grown."

"Thank you, Miss," I reply. "It's an honor to hear you say that."

"You should be proud." She steps outside, nibbling on her cookie and sipping her tea. "The community loves this little nook."

The bell above the door jingles faintly behind her. I turn back to the counter, taking a breath as I put away the last few tins of tea, restocking the inventory one by one.

My phone vibrates on the counter. It's a message from Sage:

*Hi sis! I'm about 20 minutes away from your shop.*

*Me: Perfect, drive safe and see you soon boo!*

I take a seat and pack up a cute package of my shop's goodies for Sage: A bundle of sage (for Sage, of course), some three-ounce packs of our best loose-leaf tea, a bottle of our small-batch olive oil, golden honey from the local apiary, and one of our new shea butter bath bombs infused with dried floral petals. I tie it together with some twine, then add a handwritten note:

*For my soul sister. I'm endlessly grateful for our sisterhood, your heart is so pure and selfless and I'm forever in awe of you. You give so much to others. I love you so much, Here's a little something just for you.*

Moments later, the bell above the door jingles. Sage walks in wearing a brown flowy dress. Her presence is grounding as warmth and peace surround her; you feel it as she enters a room. She always wears a calm and confident smile, light brown eyes beaming, and her blonde locs gathered high and loose with some gold jewelry catching the light.

Sage and I met a few years ago when I was still living in Florida. We had mutual friends, and ended up staying at the same Brickell hotel for a weekend. Our story starts with an elevator meet-cute— one of those unexpected moments that clicks instantly. Since then, we've been locked in, and years later she's one of my closest friends.

"Hiiiiii, babyyyy!" I look up and immediately break into a jog.

"Hayyy, sis!" She laughs, catching me with ease.

"Miaaaa!" She beams, and says, "You tackle people like you're in a rom-com!"

"Oh my gosh, it's been too long! Can you blame me?" You look so good, sis!! Where's the hubby?"

"Off being social meeting up with an old friend from his LA days. So I get you all to myself." She steps further in and takes it all in, the soft lighting, the wooden shelves lined with jars, the flower bundles drying near the windows. Her expression stills for a moment.

"Mia...it's beautiful. You really did it." That soft praise always gets me. I hand her the little gift bag.

"For me?" she asks eagerly.

"Open it." She reads the note and smiles at me.

"You're so thoughtful, sis!"

Life's been moving fast—between her creative projects and my whirlwind days at the shop, Sage and I have had little time to catch up. We usually catch up on FaceTime, given that she lives on the East Coast. She and her husband planned a vacation to California, and during the vacation they coordinated lunch. She's been in my life for a few years now, and her presence has always felt sacred. She's a full-time content creator and author, but more than that—Sage is someone who leads with spirit. Ever since her mother passed a couple of years ago, she's honored her in such intentional ways. The way she weaves grief into gratitude, how she shares her reflections—it's nothing short of beautiful. Her posts feel like soul check-ins: thoughtful and grounding, much like poetry. Somehow they always arrive just when you need them. Like every word she gives nourishes something in you. I always joke that Sage is a walking love letter—she pours into the people she loves without hesitation, like it's second nature. With Sage, you feel seen. Held. Uplifted. She quotes her mother often, even in casual conversations, even when she's giving her friend's advice. She often says that the good parts of her come from her mother.

"Alright," she says, looping her arm through mine, "I want all the tea. Catch me up on everything going on in your life—I've got so much to share, too. But first—real quick—I baked you some fresh cupcakes!" I grin. Of course she did. We settle at the back table, where the light pours in and the teapot steams between us.

"I really am so thankful you two made this stop in the middle of your vacation," I say, already unwrapping a cupcake. "I love our FaceTime calls, but girl—I missed you so much. Tell me how you've been? You're like glowing!"

"Mia," she says, eyes soft, "I'm wonderful. Truly happy. And actually... part of the reason I flew out here was because I've been keeping something. I've been waiting to tell you in person." I pause mid-bite. Slowly put the cupcake down and look at her, my eyes wide. She just smiles.

"Oh my gosh, Sage...are you—?"

"YES!" she nods, practically glowing.

I let out a scream of joy and hop out of my chair, wrapping her in the tightest hug. "OH MY GOSH, SAGE!" Tears rush to my eyes without warning.

"That's the most beautiful news I've heard all week. This...this just made my entire month."

"Thank you, sis! I still can't believe I'm carrying a life, I'm just full with so much gratitude." She hugs me back, and when we sit down again, there's a tenderness in her expression. "I keep thinking about my mom," she says quietly. "How I'm becoming someone's mother now... It's surreal." I reach for her hand.

"She's with you, Sage. You know that, right?" She nods.

"All the time. When I found out, it was raining. You know, my mother comes to me in the rain."

"I believe that. Completely. She's been with you every step, Sage. Of course, she'd show up for this moment. A new life...her grandbaby." I reach out to hold her hand gently.

"Thank you. You're such a true and valued friend to me."

"You never need to thank me, please! I'm just so happy I got to hear this from you in person, I'm honored that you're sharing this with me. I'm so excited to see your belly when you begin to show!"

"You're so sweet, sis. I've been taking polaroid pictures every two weeks to track my belly. Anyway, enough about me and my little bean. What's been going on with you?"

She leans forward, eyes gleaming with curiosity.

"Who's this mystery man you've been conveniently vague about on the phone?"

"Oh, please," I laugh, brushing her off. "He's a sweetheart. Makes me laugh a lot. Very fun to look at. But...it's nothing serious. At least—I don't think either of us is looking at it that way. It's also still early." Sage raises her brow but says nothing.

"We both know he's on contract out here; he's a travel RN. Everything about him being here feels temporary. So, I don't know...I guess I'm just looking at it like a summer thing as I've been enjoying his company." I swirl the tea in my cup, avoiding her gaze for a second too long. Sage looks at me for a few moments in silence but there's no judgment in her face—just that quiet knowing she always seems to carry.

"A summer thing, huh?" she repeats. "Okay...but I also know you, Mia. And I can clearly see how you light up talking about him." I give her a look, but she just smiles and shrugs.

"I'm not saying it has to be serious. It's still early, I get that. But sometimes, the things we write off as temporary? They end up sticking around in ways we didn't expect." She reaches for her matcha then. "Just...don't write off what you feel just because of a timeline. That's all I'm saying." I sigh, half-smiling.

"Leave it to you to make me rethink everything over cupcakes." I say as I lick the frosting off of one. Sage grins.

"You know that's my brand."

We grab our matcha to stroll down the street, chatting about everything and nothing—her children's book, the baby moon she's planning in Costa Rica. I tell her I'm thinking about getting back into pole dancing more regularly. We laugh about how we've both been experimenting in the kitchen lately—me with my ube cookies, and her with ice cream from scratch. A few blocks over, we duck into a tiny boutique with hand-stitched baby clothes and wooden mobiles. I pick up a romper shaped like a strawberry to send her home with. Not long after, her husband pulls up to get her. We pull each other in for a tight, loving embrace.

"See you on FaceTime soon, sissy. I love you so much!"

"I love you! Thank you for my gifts. I appreciate you so much," she says, eyes glowing.

"Girl, of course. We could go in circles with our love and gratitude. Safe travels, boo!"

She laughs as she heads to the car, the strawberry romper tucked under her arm. Her husband Josiyah gets out the car to open the car door for her but greets her first with a forehead kiss and a cute butt tap. Their love is truly so beautiful, and poetic—a marriage people pray for and dream of. When they walk into a room you feel it. He treasures her deeply. He turns to me and greets me with a sincere smile.

"It's good to see you, Mia!" he says. "I've heard great things are happening with the shop. Congrats!"

"Thank you so much, friend!" They get in the car and waves goodbye to me. I wave back with a smile, and watch them go—already missing her.

Right on cue, a text comes in:

*Khalid: Hey beautiful, how was your time with your friend?*

*Me: Hey love, it was incredible. I missed her so much, she just left with her hubby.*

*Khalid: I'm happy to hear that. Would you like to go out this evening?*

*Me: I'd like that. What did you want to get into?*

*Khalid: Let's grab dinner and if you're up for it head to Santa Monica Pier for some games?*

*Me: I'd love that. Let's go whoop yo ass in some games.*

*Khalid: Now here you go. lol Careful, I don't like embarrassing people in public! Does 7 work for you? I don't want you to feel rushed.*

*Me: 7 is perfect.*

I glance up and I feel myself smiling out of excitement. Sage gives me something to think about. *What if, by the end of his contract, this was more?*

# CHAPTER SIX
## *Khalid*

I stare at my phone, cheesing. Babygirl has that best-friend type of vibe. Before heading back to my Airbnb after my work meeting, I stop at the small neighborhood store to pick up some flowers. I scan the different bouquets, some with smaller rose heads, others with a mix of sizes. I hesitate, Mia does this for a living and carries weight in her local community because of it. I hope I'm not about to embarrass myself. I continue to stare at the selection. Most are fine, but then I come across one that's nearly in full bloom—each petal rich, deep red. I lift it carefully. Even without a vase, it feels alive, deliberate, like it was meant for her. They have to be beautiful. I grab it, and the store associate pops them in a brown paper bag for me to hold on the ride home. I head back, start the shower, and let the hot water hit, loosening the tension from the day.

I glance down at myself—beard and haircut freshly lined up, light fitted jeans and a crisp white shirt, sleeves casually rolled, golds in my mouth, the hint of a strong frame showing just enough without being showy. Flowers in hand, I head her way to pick her up.

"Hey love, oh my gosh—Aww! Khalid, are those for me?"

"Who else would they be for?" I say, smiling, pulling her in for a kiss.

"Thank you, love," she says. She sets them on the bench next to her door inside.

"I'll put them in water when we get back. Let's go, I'm starving!"

"Lead the way, ma'am!" I say.

We hop on my bike and I notice how she does it so naturally now as she's been on it a few times. She wraps her arms at my sides and like they're supposed to be there. She rests her head on my back, I start the engine and we ride off.

*

The evening flows seamlessly between us. We hit up a taco spot for dinner and drinks as we trade stories about our week. Her, catching up with her homegirl, her shop, and my work days at the hospital. The way she listens and asks questions almost catches me off guard, she's actually intrigued by my day. I can't remember the last time I was with anyone who asked about me like this before Mia. Not out of obligation, but genuine interest and care. By the time we finish up, the sky has darkened but the Pier is alive. More jokes are cracked, having us laughing the whole time, trading Ls and wins back and forth.

"Man, we didn't get it on camera, so technically it didn't happen." I joke after she steals another game from me. She laughs.

"Khalid, shut up! You better let me have my win!".

"I'm messing with you, you got me real good a few times."

We finally head toward a bench overlooking the water. She's clutching the oversized teddy bear I won her. She glances at me, "Have you ever seen *Soul*?" I shake my head.

"Nah, not yet. That's the Pixar one?"

"Yeah," she says, her face softening. "You gotta watch it. It's so good, I'd watch it again. It hits differently when you're older, you know?"

"What did you like about it so much?" I ask. She thinks for a second, eyes on the water.

"I guess...it reminds you to slow down, life isn't about one big moment. And if you only focus on a big grand moment, you'll miss out on life in between. I always try to remember gratitude in every aspect of my life, even the small moments. For instance, finding five bucks on the floor, or being near this beautiful body of water and being able to witness it. It keeps me grounded. So any reminder of that—even in a Pixar movie—is special to me."

I nod, quiet for a moment, because it's not what I expected her to say. There's something real about the way she says it—*simple*, but it sticks.

We reach the bench and sit, the pier lights stretching across the water like little constellations. I glance at her and the teddy bear sitting on her lap.

"Do you feel like you're living life to the fullest right now?" She hums softly.

"Hmmm, yeah, I think so. I've slowed down a lot. I stop forcing myself into rooms that weren't meant for me. I used to measure myself only by milestones and acceptance, standards that were really never my own, it limited me." I watch her for a moment, the way she says speaks her truth. She continues.

"My mother taught me to recognize early on when a space is welcoming or when it's merely tolerating you, the lesson has stayed with me as I've navigated my adult life. Now in my thirties, I'm learning to just be. To take up space without shrinking. " She pauses and looks at me.

"What about you?" I take a moment to process what she's saying before responding.

"Yeah I do. Lately I've actually felt like life's just starting again for me. Even at thirty-four." I glance out at the water. She settles beside me, tucking her knees closer to her chest.

"It's such a privilege to have the opportunity to rebuild yourself and change your story." she adds.

"I agree, I feel blessed." I turn to her and nudge her arm.

"When can I see you again?"

"You tryin' real hard to make this a habit, huh?" She teases.

"Aye, I don't see an issue but I can let up!" I say jokingly.

"No, don't!" She laughs, then asks, "How about Friday?"

"Friday it is. I leave the next morning for Florida, but I'd love to see you before I go." I pull her closer, her laughter quieting against my chest.

"Okay, also I can take you to the airport. Dinner again?" she asks, looking up at me, eyes searching mine for something I can already feel forming between us. I meet her gaze, leaning in until there's barely air between us.

"Thank you and I want to try something different. Let me come up with something." I kiss her at the end of my sentence and lock eyes with her.

"Okay. I trust ya. I know we will have a time regardless." I brush a hand along her back, memorizing the moment.

"Come on," I say quietly. "Let me get you home. You've got an early morning at the shop." She nods, clutching the teddy bear against her chest as we walk. Her fingers slip into mine like they belong there. The night is peaceful around us—low lights, ocean breeze, and that unspoken thing growing between us.

We walk back to my motorcycle, and as we do, I can't help thinking about Friday. It's only a couple of days away, but it feels like forever. I already know I'm gonna be counting down every hour until I see her again.

We make our way back to her place and I walk her to her front porch. I lean in and press a gentle kiss to her forehead. Before I can pull back, she looks up at me, I brush a thumb along her jaw and kiss her once, lightly, but she meets me halfway the second time—warm, and unhurried. She reaches for my hand, guiding it gently to her waist. I take the silent invitation and let my palm rest there, tracing the curve of her hip as we taste each other's lips. When we finally part, she lets out a quiet laugh, one that lingers in her voice.

"Goodnight, Khalid."

"Goodnight, Mia," I say.

She slips inside, still smiling, and I stand there long enough to watch the light flick on through her window before I head back to my bike.

Back at the Airbnb, I drop my keys on the counter, shower and start packing up my things—laying out my stuff for tomorrow's work day, and folding some clothes for my trip into my carry-on bag, making sure everything's set for the flight to South Florida. I don't need to take much, given that I still have a closet with some clothing there, but I still want to make sure I'm ready. Friday's only two days away, and it barely counts anyway. Between work and taking Mia out, time's already spoken for.

I pull a clean pair of scrubs from the drawer and lay them out for tomorrow, then pat my pockets for my wallet. When I spot it on the nightstand and pick it up, something slips out—a small, worn photo of my grandfather and me holding coconuts we got from the tree in his backyard. I flip it around and see the date in faded ink: *July 2005. Damn,* I reminisce, *I was eleven years old then.*

His being gone still feels unreal. I gently put the picture back in my wallet just as I feel my eyes get hot.

*I'm going to visit his grave no matter what.*

I won't leave Florida without doing so.

*

I pull into the West Fitness parking lot just before noon. Through the glass, I spot James already inside, warming up near the free weights. I down my pre-workout, grab my water bottle, and head in.

"Yo!" James calls out, lifting a hand as I walk up. "Thought you were gonna leave me hangin', man."

"Nah," I laugh, dapping him up. "You said you wanted to train like you mean it. I came to hold you to it."

We hit the bench area, loading plates and trading warm-up tips. The convo's easy. I didn't come to LA looking for friendships, but James is solid. Between sets, I check my phone. There's a text from Mia.

*Mia: I made some cookies and cream Rice Krispy treats for the shop and they SOLD OUT!*

*Me: Of course they did. They sound like they slap—you've gotta let me try one.*

James leans over, pretending not to be nosy but nosy, anyway.

"Oh okay, bro! Got you a lil' shorty on the West Coast? That's cool." I slide my phone back into my pocket.

"She's beautiful, man. Real cool, too. I'm just getting to know her." Then I hear her.

"Oh wow, look who's here."

I glance over my shoulder. *Sierra.* Dressed in a matching set, with styled hair and a full face of makeup, like she's headed to a sponsored shoot instead of a workout. Green juice in one hand, phone in the other. James raises an eyebrow.

"You told Sierra?" I shake my head.

"Nope." She walks up casually, like she owns the place.

"Figured I'd check it out—get a feel for the place." She looks directly at me. "Since you're such a fan."

"Didn't realize word spread that fast," I respond, keeping my tone neutral.

"It's LA," she says knowingly. "Word spreads with GPS pins and hashtags."

James lets out a low chuckle and drifts toward the treadmills, probably on purpose. Sierra leans against the barbell rack.

"So...how's your day going?"

"It's good," I say lightly. "Just here to get some reps in. How's your day going?" She tilts her head, like she's waiting for a reaction.

"It's been great, had my morning coffee before coming to meet you boys. You're different outside of work."

"Different how?" I ask, eyes on the plates.

"Focused. Kinda quiet. Mysterious, maybe." She sips her juice. "It's a vibe." She pauses then. "Khalid, I didn't know you wear golds, they looks so clean. I also have a pair!"

"Oh cool, cool, yeah they're really popular in Florida." As the words leave my mouth, I think: *None of this conversation feels real. It's all just... basic. Predictable.* I can't stop myself from drifting on autopilot, offering the shortest possible responses as a default. She's still lingering around me but somewhat dancing to the music in her headphones. I wrap my hands around the bar.

"So what are you going to work out today?" She watches me a little too long.

"Probably legs and glutes. Just warming up to this playlist. Are we gonna do a workout together or...?"

"I'm training with James today, and we're working on our back and chest. We already mapped it out." Something shifts in her demeanor for a second, but she smooths it over like it never happened. She turns and walks off toward the squat rack, a little more posture in her step than before. James returns a few minutes later with two towels, tossing me one.

"She came dressed for cardio, but I don't think she's here to sweat." I laugh under my breath.

"She's cool. Just...*persistent.*" James chuckles.

"Anyway, whatchu got planned for tomorrow?"

"Got a date." Sierra must've been listening, because her head whips around from the machine like she just heard an alarm.

"A date?" she asks, eyebrows raised like I betrayed her. "I didn't know you were dating!" I raise a brow.

"Didn't realize I was reporting to you." She blinks, caught off guard, then recovers with a tight laugh.

"I mean, it's just news. You've been moving real lowkey, that's all."

"Yeah," I say, keeping it easy. "Trying to keep good things close." James lets out a low whistle.

"That's right, my boy tryna cuff a shorty on the West Coast!" I shake my head, laughing.

"Relax. It's new." Sierra crosses her arms, unreadable.

"Well, I hope you both have a good time. She nods slowly, eyes lingering like she wants to say more—but doesn't. She turns and heads back toward the machines, and just like that, the tension lifts. James mutters under his breath, clearly entertained.

"Yeah, bro, you definitely got fans out here."

"I'm not here for that," I say. He nods, serious now.

"Respect. And for what it's worth—it shows." My phone buzzes again. Mia.

*Mia: I'll make a second batch and put some aside for you :)*

*Me: Thank you. I can't wait to see you, babygirl.*

Everything else fades.

"All right," I say, locking in. "Let's work."

*

We finish up a little after two. I dap James up in the lot, promising we'll link up again soon. Sierra gives us both a quick goodbye—at this point, I'm sure she gets it. I swing a leg over my bike and straddle the seat, helmet balanced on the mirror while I check my phone. When I pull up outside my Airbnb, my phone lights up. Hakeem. I prop it on the tank and hit accept on the FaceTime before I kill the engine.

"Look who finally remembered he got a brother!" he chimes, cheesing from his room. Same old wall posters. Same old him.

"Man, chill. Been working." I say, smiling.

"Working...and what else?" He narrows his eyes. "You got a lil' something out there, don't you?" I laugh under my breath.

"Maybe. Nothing crazy. She cool people though. I'm taking her out tonight." I say casually. He raises his eyebrows, grinning widely.

"Ahh, okay! I see you, bro!"

"Aye, how's Mom?" I ask, leaning back. His face softens a bit.

"She's good. Been cooking again, working on the house like before. Keeps asking when you coming home."

"Cool, cool. I'm packed up for my flight. I know it's only a few days, but it will be nice to see everyone again." Hakeem nods, satisfied with my short home visit.

"Say less. Send me your flight info—I'll scoop you from the airport. No Uber, bro, I got you."

"Bet. Appreciate you."

"For real though, mom's gonna lose her mind seeing you. She misses you." Just then, her voice cuts in from the background.

"IS THAT MY SON?".

"Hey, Ma!"

"Hi, baby! How are you? You being safe? Those earthquakes didn't get you, did they?" She teases, half-serious. I laugh.

"I'm good. Promise. Just working and staying out of the way." She squints at the camera.

"Mmhmm. You eating enough? Learn how to cook yet?" I roll my eyes but can't stop smiling.

"I'm eating, Ma."

"Good—you better be! When you get here, I got some projects around the house I need your help with!" Hakeem cracks up in the background.

"Damn, you just gonna put me straight to work?" She laughs, playful as ever.

"Who else gon' do it? Not your daddy, that's for sure!" I grin.

"Love you Ma, I'll see you soon."

"You better," she says, pretending to pout. "I love you too son." My mom passes the phone back to Hakeem.

"I'm all set though," I say to Hakeem "and this girl I've been talking to out here... she's taking me to the airport." Hakeem raises his eyebrows.

"You talking to someone out there? Shit, I need to hear about this!"

"Man, chill!" I say, barely able to fight my smile when it comes to Mia.

"Alright bro, see you tomorrow. Don't have me out there waiting while you FaceTiming your girl from baggage claim." I shake my head, laughing.

"Man, alright see you soon bro!" He laughs too, then drops his voice, sincerely.

"Bet. Talk soon, bro."

I hang up, slip my helmet back on, and catch my reflection in the side mirror—smiling from ear to ear. She hasn't laughed like that in a while. I head inside, kick my shoes off by the door, and let the day roll off me. A hot shower hits just right—steam filling up the bathroom while I run the clippers through my hair, cleaning myself up good. Back on the couch, towel around my neck, I scroll mindlessly through Instagram until a flyer catches my eye—dim lights, old records, velvet chairs. A poetry bar tucked in some corner of town I've never been to. I feel like she'd like this.

I tap the reservation I made for a different restaurant and cancel it without a second thought. This spot feels special. And she's...different. I wanna do this right. Especially since I'm dipping out to Florida tomorrow. One real good night before I leave town for a few days. Something she'll remember. I lean back, a grin tugging at my lips. Yeah. Tonight's going to be special.

*Me: Hey, for tonight wear whatever makes you feel good. It's dressy, but not over the top. I'll be at your crib by seven.*

A minute later, her bubbles pop up.

*Mia: Mmm, a mystery? I like surprises. Seven it is.*

# CHAPTER SEVEN
## *Mia*

Khalid pulls up to my place just before sunset with another beautiful bouquet of flowers, this time full bloom peonies. He's fresh—skin glowing, beard lined up, and a fresh cut. His tattoos look like jewelry. The way his eyes linger when he sees me tells me I got it right tonight. For a heartbeat, I wish this night could stretch longer than it will before he's off to Florida for a few days. My hair is big—my curls are defined to perfection, full of volume, bounce, and confidence. I'm wearing a fitted olive green two-piece: a strapped crop top that shows just enough skin and a high-slit skirt that flows when I walk. Gold chains around my waist and my belly ring glints in the golden light. Gold hoops, a dainty gold necklace with a white crystal, and a few stacked rings complete the look. I feel like summer magic.

"You look..." he pauses, exhaling through a smile. "Yeah. You look amazing."

"Thank you." I say. "You look so handsome," I say as I cup the back of his neck with my hands and tippy-toe for a kiss. He then hands me the flowers.

"I know you own a floral shop, always making arrangements for everyone else. You should still have flowers picked out just for you," he says, his voice above a whisper.

"You're so sweet to me," I gush, as I start to sit on the passenger side while he holds my car door open.

He doesn't move right away—just watches me smiling with a quiet hunger he doesn't always say out loud. We begin our drive and I put on some slow and soulful R&B from the '90s, he glances over and grins like I'm predictable in the best way. He takes me to a romantic poetry bar disguised as a library. When we step inside, it smells like cedar wood and incense. The lighting is low, warm; it's romantic. The walls are lined with shelves that contain vintage books, wrapping the space in art and soul. Candles flicker on small round tables, and soft jazz hums in the air amidst the low conversations.

"I found this place by accident," Khalid leans in and whispers in my ear. "Thought of you instantly." I glance up at him and pull him in for a kiss.

"It's perfect." We find a table near the stage. The host gives a quick nod, and we order some drinks and small bites. I watch him as he watches the stage—relaxed, focused, with that signature tilt of his head when he's taking something in deeply.

"Do you ever get up and perform?" I ask, teasing, sipping from my glass. He grins.

"Nah, that is not my calling, but I enjoy the art of it."

I laugh, but then the lights dim a little more, and someone steps up to the mic. A Trinidadian woman in a floor-length purple dress with locs piled on top of her head. As she begins to speak, the room falls silent. She speaks of love—of building it, shaping it, with someone you found. I feel moved. Almost emotional.

Khalid doesn't look at me while she's reading, but I feel him.

The way his fingers brush the inside of my wrist. The way his knee presses gently into mine. And when the poem ends, he turns to me like he's been waiting to stare at me longingly.

"Wow," he whispers.

"That was beautiful," I reply.

"So are you."

He lifts my hand and kisses it. I look away, smiling, flustered. But under the table, my hand slides into his. We take a selfie together for my memory, knowing he's leaving tomorrow even though it's only for a few days. I post it on my Instagram story, knowing our time together is fleeting, but I do it anyway and to my surprise he posted it on his too.

The night continues.

Another poet takes the mic. This time a Black man, who talks about the first time he laid eyes on his wife and how knew he would marry her. He speaks about how sacred marriage is. Then, the bartender brings a fresh candle to our table. Watching the candle flicker, a warmth spreads in my body. I have a sudden fleeting thought of the same candle glow beside my bed, and the two of us curled into each other under my sheets. I feel my cheeks blush at the thought. I lean my head against Khalid's shoulder, and he lets it stay there. The entire night, our interaction feels...*effortless.*

Later, when we walk to the car, the night continues to carry the romance. The moon is full, and the air feels warm. Even though we're not in the holiday season, there's twinkling lights in the trees around us. He opens the passenger door and leans against it, eyes on me like he's memorizing the moment.

"I don't want to end the night yet," he says.

"Well...Destiny's at her man's house for the night. Want to come over?" He grins like I just made his night.

"Lead the way."

The drive is simple, fun—we're cracking up like two teenagers. At some point, I kick off my shoes and tuck one leg under me.

"You really listen to ASMR?" he asks, eyes on the road, smirking. I gasp dramatically.

"You make that sound like a crime." He laughs.

"I just don't get how whispering and tapping on random stuff is supposed to be relaxing."

"It's soothing! You have no imagination."

"Okay, but the brushing-the-mic-with-a-makeup-brush thing? You can't tell me that's not weird."

"Says the grown man with a *Dragon Ball Z* addiction and a favorite anime opening theme."

"That's different. Anime builds character." I roll my eyes.

"You had a Naruto headband, didn't you?" He looks genuinely offended.

"First of all—yes. But that's not the point." He laughs again. I shake my head, laughing.

"I'm messing with you. Believe it or not, my favorite movie is an anime—*Spirited Away*." He whips his head toward me.

"Stop lying!"

"I'm so serious!" I say, hands up like I'm swearing it. "That movie had me in a chokehold. I used to pretend I was Chihiro every time I walked past a public bathhouse." He bursts out laughing.

"Okay, see, now I gotta make you a watch list. You lowkey got taste." His hand stays on my thigh across the console, casually, like it's second nature.

# CHAPTER EIGHT
## *Khalid*

We arrive back at her townhouse. Her place smells like lavender the second I step inside. It fits her. Warm, soft, a little wild in the corners with pictures everywhere of her and her sisters, all smiling, arms draped over each other like they don't know how to be anything but close. She slips off her shoes by the door, then puts on her house slippers to walk on the wood floors, still laughing at something I said on the way up the stairs. I don't even remember what it was—I'm too busy watching her.

"Mia, your place is beautiful. It's warm...like you."

She looks back at me with a calm smile, settling in.

"Thank you! Oh—wait," she says, as she heads into the kitchen. She returns with a small container. "I saved you one. Cookies and Cream Rice Krispy treat. I didn't forget." My face lights up like a kid.

"I knew you were the one." She laughs, curling up on the couch as I take the first bite and I shake my head amazed at how delicious it is.

"That good?"

"Better than good," I say, mouth full. "You could probably sell these for emotional support." We talk and sip, stretched out in her living room, the energy still flirty. At some point, I get the idea in my head that I want to see pictures of her from when she was younger, and after a few insistent requests, she gives in and retrieves a small photo album from her drawer.

"Oh my goodness, fine—but don't make fun of me. While some folks called them 'dookey braids,' I firmly believe my pigtails and bobos' was killin' the game back in the day!" she says while cheesing, handing over a small album. I flip open the cover and nearly choke on my drink.

"Babe!" I grin, shaking the photo like it's a Polaroid picture. "You've gotta let me keep this. In fact I'm not asking, you just not getting it back."

"See, you actin' real bold for someone sitting in my living room!" she yells back.

"I didn't hear anything you just said, but I'm making it your contact photo, right now." I say as I snap a photo of the photograph with my phone.

"Khalid! I don't know who pays you to be this annoying!"

"God, probably," I say with a smug sip. "Direct deposit every Friday."

We laugh until we're both breathless, sprawled across her rug with photo evidence of her baby cheeks and crooked pigtails between us. The conversation shifts easily from stories from our childhoods, college memories, brief moments we haven't thought of in years. We eat ice cream straight from the pint and take turns picking the next song; it playing low in the background.

"So you actually sat next to Pretty Ricky's girlfriend in college?" She asks, grinning.

"Yeah," I say, smirking. "And I had these little tattoos on my wrist. Thought I was the man in the classroom. Every chance I got, I'd hand her a pencil with the hand that had the tattoo. Raise my hand with the tattoos—subtle, right?" She keeps laughing, holding up her hands as if pretending to be me.

"Aye, you know we chillin' or whatever!" I can hardly breathe.

"Exactly! But then one day, I tried to flash my tiny wrist tattoos in front of my cousin from Atlanta, and he just yanks up his shirt and goes, 'Don't make me pull these sheets out on you, boy.' This man had a chest and stomach completely covered in ink. Yo, I felt like a toddler showing off stickers." We double over then, tears in our eyes from laughing so much. Later, I rub her feet while she leans back, eyes half closed, sipping the last of her wine. I don't even notice how late it's gotten until the clock on her stove reads nearly midnight.

"Khalid," she says quietly. "I still don't want this night to end."

I glance up. "I don't either, Mia."

I lean in to kiss her and gently rub her back, feeling the warmth of her skin under her shirt. She places her hands on my neck and pulls me in closer. I can feel both of our heart rates speeding up. I want her. I want every part of her. I could get lost in this moment with her and be perfectly fine. Our kisses get deeper, and our breathing gets heavier. The world fades away, leaving only the taste of her lips and the undeniable pull we share. I gently pick her up and take her to her bedroom. Our lips still connected as I set her on her bed. We take each other's shirts off slowly to soak in this moment further. I climb on top of her and begin kissing her down her chest to her navel. I slide my hands under the fabric of her skirt and run my fingers down her hips to her thighs, pulling it off. My hands explore her body as our lips meet again. She moans against my lips as I gently tease her bottom one between my teeth. She removes the buckle from my belt. I sit up between her legs to remove my pants. I place her right leg on my shoulder and start kissing it, making my way down to taste her. Her back arches as she throws her head back in pure pleasure. Making our connection deeper,  I take my time with my tongue licking her clit, kissing her center lips, her body inches up and I pull her waist back to me. Her moan escalates as her legs shiver. I pause, savoring the moment before slowly retracing my path upward to kiss her neck. She guides me by wrapping her legs around me and pulls me in closer, her body pressing against mine with an urgency that mirrors my own.

She grabs my dick and rubs her clit with it, teasing us both as the tip dips in and out of her just slightly. I look her in the eyes and she bites her lip. I take the invitation and melt into her slowly. Tight and wet, her gasps are instant as I stretch her. Each stroke tells her the truth: I want all of this, all of her. She moans louder,  and I pull her closer. Our foreheads press together and we keep going, kissing in between, each stroke more intense than the last. The sight of us tangled together nearly undoes me— dicking her down, with nothing on other than her gold chain draped across her chest, the rush of goodness overwhelms me. As I'm kissing her I start to work my way to her chest and I gently cup her breast to lick her nipples slowly as I'm thrusting. Her moan intensifies, and after a few more strokes,  she bites my shoulder then lets out a scream.

We've peaked in our pleasure. And with that, we lay still, holding each other. I gently play with her curls while she strokes my beard. The moonlight seeping through the cracks of her windows allows us to lock eyes. Silent communication happens that speaks volumes without a single word uttered. The contract comes to mind, but right now I pretend like it doesn't exist. I don't want this moment with her to end. Within minutes, sleep finds her. I watch her sleep for a few minutes longer, memorizing her face. I know better than to wish for forever, but damn...if I don't want it, anyway.

# CHAPTER NINE
## *Mia*

I wake up warm—his arm still heavy across my waist, like a missing puzzle piece. It felt so natural I didn't move at first. Just let myself melt into the stillness, into him. He's still asleep, breathing slowly and evenly, as if he had nowhere else to be.

I shift slightly and feel him stir behind me. He mumbles something low in my hair and pulls me in tighter.

"Morning," I whisper, smiling.

"Mm. Five more minutes," he rasps.

I stay there. We don't need to say much. His presence alone is louder than words. Eventually, I turn over to face him.

"Are you hungry?" I ask.

"Starving," he mumbles, pressing his lips to my shoulder, his voice thick with sleep. "But not just for food." I roll my eyes and smacked him with the pillow beside me. He grins. "You got pancake mix?" he asks with eyes still closed, his voice husky from the sleep.

"I think I do, actually."

"Alright, bet," he says, stretching as he sits up. "Let me make you breakfast."

A smile spreads across my face. "Okay."

*

I sit cross-legged on the couch, wrapped in my favorite throw blanket, while he moves through my kitchen as though he's been here a dozen times. My heart soaks up this moment, greedy. And for half a second, I can't stand myself for wanting this so badly. I should know better. I shake my head to clear my thoughts.

"Where'd you learn to cook?" I call out.

"My mom," he answers. "If I wanna make a woman happy, I gotta learn how to cook."

"Smart woman." I retort. "Tell me more about her," I demand softly, as I watch him flip a pancake in the pan.

"She's kind. Always throwing a house party. Very social and sweet. Hardworking. She does all the house projects herself, we joke constantly about getting her a tool belt. Summer dress, hand-held drill, and fanny pack with all her tools—that's her outfit all summer while she's working on projects around the house. Always helping people, always busy."

"She sounds like a force of nature. I like that."

"Yes, she's one of those people who can make you feel capable and ridiculous at the same time. You never know whether to thank her or apologize for being lazy." He turns toward me with a plate of fluffy golden pancakes in his hands. I take a moment to really look at him. His smooth brown skin catches the morning light, muscles flexing slightly with each step. It isn't just how he looks—it's the way he moves toward me, like I was something to take care of.

"Try it with this," he says, holding out a small pitcher.

"What is it?"

"It's a peanut butter syrup I made. You'll like it—promise." I pour it on the pancakes he plated for me just to humor him—the first bite is delicious.

"Oh my God," I mumble through a mouthful. "That's actually incredible."

"Told you," he says. I chuckle as I take more bites.

"Wait, where's your plate?" He smiles at me. Then he reaches for the plate in my hand and gently slides it away from me.

"Wait, what are you—" I start, laughing as he sets it aside, but something in his eyes makes my words trail off. He kneels in front of me, hands warm on my thighs, and slowly begins tugging the blanket away.

"I just fed you," he responds, voice low. "Now it's my turn to eat." Heat blooms across my chest, spreading downward.

"Khalid—" I barely whisper, "you have a flight, we have to leave—"

"Don't worry about that." he murmurs, his fingers slipping beneath my shorts to slide them off. "Let me." I don't even try to talk back. I close my eyes, and let out a soft breath as his hand feels on me gently while kissing me. Then slowly he works his way down my body, teasing me kissing my thighs like he has all the time in the world. He starts going down on me. A moan escapes me as I feel his lips against my center. His makes out with my lips, and I feel his tongue tasting me over and over again, deeper each time and I moan louder. He does it a few more times, and he stops.

"I wanna be inside you," he says, barely louder than a whisper.

"I'm all yours," I say. He takes off his boxers and moves inside me. He enters me, he feels so good, I unintentionally let my eyes roll back and bite my lip.

"God dayum, baby," he murmurs.

"Don't stop," I demand.

He keeps going, and I can't stop myself from clenching his dick each stroke is long, slow and stretches me. I cup that back of his neck with my hand and wrap my thighs around him, needing the closeness as he kisses my neck. He slides his hand down my back and grabs my ass and lifts me slightly on each thrust like he knows exactly how much I can take. "Baby!" I gasp—too loud and too honest I yell as he brings me to orgasm mid-stroke. After that, he lays between my legs kissing my navel, worshipping my body.

"You're so precious to me," he admits.

I smile and cover my face with a throw blanket. It hits me all of a sudden, then: how foreign this feels—being the priority. I've spent years performing, pretending, teaching men how to please me and still walking away unsatisfied. I used to fake it just to get it over with, just to protect their pride. But with him, there's no act, no guessing. I don't feel like I have to shrink or guide or explain. He just knows—and the way he moves makes me believe he always will.

# CHAPTER TEN
## *Khalid*

I zip up my duffel and glance around Mia's room one last time, already feeling the weight of leaving her. My hoodie is half-on as I step into the living room, and there she is—by the door, keys in hand, eyes tender but guarded. Like she doesn't want to rush me, but we both know our time is up.

"Are you ready?" she asks.

"Yeah, I think I've got everything." We walk out together. I load my bag into the backseat while she climbs into the driver's side. As we pull away from the curb, I rest my hand on her thigh. She smiles while keeping her eyes on the road.

"I want to see my family, but I don't want to leave you," I say quietly. Her hand finds mine and squeezes.

"I know, but I really want you to see your family too. Your mom will be so happy to see you. Also, I know you mentioned visiting your grandpa." I look at her as warmth spreads in my chest, realizing she remembered.

Our conversation during the ride is minimal. It isn't an awkward silence—it's the kind that holds too much. My flight is in an hour. I'm cutting it close, but I don't care; I just want a few more minutes with her.

*At least I have only a carry-on with me.*

When we pull up to the terminal, I don't move right away. I sit there studying her face, admiring her curls.

"I'll be back before you can miss me too much."

"You're already late," she whispers against my lips.

"I'll text you as soon as I land," I say, rubbing my nose against hers giving her little kisses in between.

"Get going, my love" she says. I grab my bag at that thought and step out of the car.

"Alright then, baby," I say as I tap the hood of her car. I blow her one more kiss as she pulls off and waves goodbye. And with that, I turn my back and head into the terminal.

*

I land a little after 8:00 p.m. and as soon as we hit the gate, I grab my phone and turn off airplane mode and take a story photo for Instagram.

Caption: *Homebound.*

Hakeem's text comes through right on cue: *"Let me know when to pull up, bro."*

When I step outside, the Florida air hits different—warm, sticky, and heavy with memory. I spot his car right away. He leans on the hood like he's in a movie, his locs piled on his head in a man-bun, arms folded, and a big smile that spreads across his face once he sees me. It's only been a few months but in that short amount of time, he's put on muscle, got a few more tattoos, and his locs have grown much longer.

"It's about time," he says, pulling me into a quick hug and pats my back.

"What's up man! You getting big bro!" I say.

"Good to see you, bro! And I'm tryin' to keep up with you!

How was your flight?"

"It was good, man, long but glad I'm here." I respond.

"Ma's been cooking since noon. Ackee and saltfish, dumplings, plantains...the whole spread."

"Say less." He pops the trunk, and I toss my duffel in. As I climb into the passenger seat, he glances over at me.

"Everybody at the house," Hakeem says, grinning. "You ready to get yo ass whooped in beer pong?" I smirk.

"Aw, that's cute. Y'all been practicing while I was gone? It's still not enough." He laughs, shaking his head. I chuckle to myself and look down to text Mia:

*Me: "Baby, I've landed. My brother just picked me up."*

Hakeem catches the look on my face and tilts his head. "This man came back in love." I shrug, still smiling.

"I made her pancakes this morning." His eyes grow wide.

"Pancakes?"

"Yeah. With peanut butter syrup." He lets out a low whistle.

"Oh yeah, that's a wrap." There's a beat of silence before he asks, "But what are you guys gonna do when the contract ends? Like, how serious is it? Do you know?" I hesitate.

"Hmmm...I don't know, man, we haven't really talked about it." I glance out the window, letting the movement of trees and neighborhoods blur past to distract me from the sudden knot in my chest. Then my phone lights up with a message.

*Mia: Hi my love. Thank you for telling me. I hope you enjoy your time with your family. We'll talk soon.*

I read it twice, thumb hovering over the screen, then place the phone face-down on my lap.

"You talked to Sharie since you left?" The question comes out casually, but I feel the tension underneath it. I shake my head.

"Nah. Not since I first got to Cali. She hit me up once—on some passive-aggressive BS. She wanted to see me, but I put an end to it; it was long overdue." Hakeem nods slowly.

"Good." But then he lets out a breath, like he's been holding something in. "I didn't wanna say anything earlier, but...Ma saw her," he adds. I turn toward him.

"What?"

"At the hair store. Said Sharie came up to her, all friendly. Talkin' like y'all were just on a break or something. Like everything was cool." I stare at him for a second, heat creeping into my chest.

"She said that to Ma?"

"Yeah, man. Like y'all just had a little space or whatever. Said she was 'giving you time.'" I scoff and look away, jaw clenched. Hakeem casts another look in my direction. "You know she's delusional, right?"

"I know," I mutter.

"Good. Don't let her mess with you; you're out here moving differently."

I nod, staring out the window again. Everything outside looks the same, but that part of my life? Dead weight that I'm not carrying it anymore. Especially not after everything between Mia and me. Hakeem turns the volume up a little on the music and we listen in silence for the rest of the drive. After fifteen minutes or so, we pull up at the house and my mind clears. I hop out of the car and head straight for the door. The second I step in, the smell hits—ackee simmering, saltfish in the air, and  sweet fried dumplings. Memory wraps around me and I know I'm home. My stomach makes it very clear that we're ready to throw down.

"Khalid!" My mom's voice rings out from the kitchen. She appears in the hallway two seconds later, apron still on. She hugs me as if it's been years.

"Son, you've gotten bigger! All that time in the gym is paying off, isn't it?!" I laugh into her shoulder.

"I'm doing alright, Ma. Learning to cook simple meals, staying focused—I'm real good." Hakeem follows behind me, already heading for the kitchen.

"Yeah, eating healthy," he chimes in. "He said he made pancakes with peanut butter syrup today." My mom raises an eyebrow at me.

"Look at you," she adds, smiling like she already had theories. I drop my bag at the foot of the stairs.

"You got a plate for me?"

"You know better than to ask," she says with a smile.

By the time I sit down to eat, more people have shown up. My siblings walk in, cheesing ready to have a game night. Ariana's holding a bottle of rum, then my youngest brother Elijah bursts through the back door with a few of our cousins holding a bag of red cups and different juices to chase the alcohol. Sometimes, it trips me out that they're both adults now. Elijah has gotten taller and cut his locs, he looks like a younger me.

"What's good, big bro!" Elijah says as he daps me up.

"Good to see you, man. I heard you're making moves with that car detailing business. I'm proud of you!"

"Oh yeah, yeah, it's picking up," Elijah responds cheerfully.

They set up a card table in the den, pull out Dominoes and Uno, and start pouring drinks: an impromptu celebration. I finish my plate, grab a red cup, and let myself settle into the noise. Before long, the house is buzzing with laughter and music, in the middle of all the chaos—Ariana yelling "Draw four, and don't argue with me!" while Elijah pretends like he's not reading the rules off his phone as if we all don't see what he's doing. Hakeem nudges me with his elbow.

"Alright, so what do you wanna do while you're out here?" he asks. "You've only got a couple of days. You tryna hit some spots or just chill?"

I lean back on the couch and stare into my drink for a second before answering.

"I want to get together with the boys," I trail off. "And I want to go see Grandpa," I mumble. Hakeem's expression softens immediately.

"Yeah?" I nod.

"I've been thinking about it a lot lately. When I first got to Cali, I thought that space would help me get my head right. It has been so far." Hakeem stays quiet, just keeps listening.

"I told myself I'd visit his grave when I was ready. And for a while, I wasn't. I didn't even want to drive past the cemetery. But now..." I pause. "I think I'm ready." Hakeem takes a sip of his drink, then nods.

"He'd be proud, bro. You're making moves and handling your business.

"I hope so," I reply. He claps me on the back.

"We'll go. Just say when."

The inside jokes continue to fill the room, along with game trash talk and music. Through all the commotion, though, I'm only thinking about one thing: Mia.

*Me: I'm missin you already.*

*Mia: Miss you too, handsome. But I really want you to be in the moment with your family. I'll be here when you get back.*

*Me: I appreciate you babygirl, have a wonderful night.*

*Mia: You as well.*

# CHAPTER ELEVEN
## *Mia*

Destiny is finishing packing her last things for her flight this evening to France when my phone rings—a FaceTime call from Prue.

"Hello!" she beams, smirking. "Y'all weren't gonna call me?" Destiny laughs.

"Oh my—wasn't that what we're doing now?"

"Mmhmm! You're lucky I love you both," Prue says, leaning into the camera. "Where's my cup?" I tilt the camera toward the kettle.

"On the way."

"Destiny, are you all packed up?" Prue asks.

"Yes! I got most of my stuff together, and a lot of the shipment went with Bryan this morning when he left to France, so while I do have an enormous suitcase, the very important stuff is out the way. I wish we could've flown together, but my itinerary came so much later than planned; the hosts waited till the last minute to book my flight."

"Oh goodness, that's annoying, but it's only one small thing within this entire trip. At least you guys fly back together. Also, I'll send you pictures of the cats daily, don't worry," I say.

"Oh my goodness, please do. I'm going to miss them so much—it might actually make me cry," Destiny says.

"I get it. They're our fur-babies," I reply.

"And Mia," Prue adds, teasing, "What about you? What's going on between you and the nurse?" A sneaky smile spreads across my face.

"We're great. Um when you left to Bryan's...we went to dinner, and then he came over and—"

"OH MY GOSH, Y'ALL DID THE NASTY!!" Destiny lets out a playful gasp, throwing her hands up.

"Wait, you didn't tell me! I've been home for hours!"

"Oh, they definitely did," Prue smirks. "That sneaky grin on her face gives it entirely away."

"We did," I say bashfully. "And Destiny—relax! I was still processing!"

"Well, how are you feeling?" Prue asks, leaning into the camera. "I mean...you look glowy."

"Shut up," I say with a chuckle. "I'm great. He's amazing. It's just...I don't know, part of me doesn't even have the words to explain how I feel. Like—he doesn't live here. Neither of us has addressed that and I think it's because we might be looking at this as just a fling? I don't know."

"Hmmp...Tèt chaje," Destiny says in Creole. "Well, he seems easy to talk to. Have you considered having a genuine conversation about it? I know he's on contract, but it's nearly six months long, and you guys have been dating basically since the beginning of the contract."

"Very true," I say, nodding. "I guess I just don't know. Part of me is like, don't overthink it, because I knew what I was getting into. I've always known he was under contract. But the other part of me didn't expect to feel this way about him. I know I like him, but...it feels deeper than that."

"When will you see each other again?" Prue asks from the FaceTime call.

"He's in Florida. I dropped him off at the airport yesterday. He'll be there for a few more days."

"You guys are both adults," Destiny says gently. "He could have the same thoughts you do, and you just don't know it."

"You could be right," I admit. "I just...I don't want to make things complicated. He came out here for a fresh start, and while I know I'm in a good place mentally, I don't want to assume that for him. Also, I can already see how easy it would be to carry more than what's mine, and though I really like him, I refuse to do that again in a relationship. I know where I stand, and Khalid is grown enough to figure out where he stands and convey that. After all, this was meant to be his reset." I say firmly.

"Destiny's right" Prue chimes in. "Though I do see where you're coming from and why you want him to initiate it. But keep in mind that not everything is black and white, Mia. With that said, if you do initiate the conversation, just make sure you're not shrinking yourself, I think that's more important."

I nod, but deep down, I don't think I'm going to. What I feel is too nuanced to blurt out—too layered to put into words without it sounding like a plea. Perhaps it's my pride. Asking a man to move cross country and stay with me...I don't know, it feels weird. I might as well get down on one knee and ask him to marry me...

*Oh, hell na. This conversation should come from him—actually it needs to.*

"But real quick—how was it?" Destiny teases cutting off my trail of thoughts.

"It was...amazing," I say, trying to stop my smiling from widening too much.

"Yes! We love a smart man who's also great in bed! That's the BD energy we want!" Destiny cheers.

"She's right, major BD energy." Prue adds. "He checks all the boxes."

"You guys are too funny, I'll think about what you said. Anyway, I hate to cut this conversation short, but we do have to get going. Destiny, you need to order your Uber to head out soon, and I need to finish getting ready. We have a shipment coming in and I have to get to the shop to sign for it, and I'll still need to shower."

"Thank you for holding it down while I'm away!" Destiny says.

"I'm happy to. Besides, it's not just me—we've got staff, so it's not overwhelming. You just make sure you got everything you before you leave, and of course kill it out there!"

"Bye ladies, love you, chat soon!" Prue says. The screen goes dark, and it's just the two of us again. Destiny finishes zipping her last suitcase and turns to me.

"Destiny! I'm going to miss you so much," I express. She stands and pulls me into a hug.

"I'm going to miss you too. We will FaceTime every chance we get!"

"I'm also, so proud of you. You've worked so hard, and this is such a big moment. Not everyone gets invited to show their art in a gallery in Paris, Destiny. Opportunities like this? They're only going to keep finding you."

"Thank you. You always know how to make me feel seen." I pull back smiling and glance at the clock. "You sure you're ready for that red-eye?"

"Please," she says, grabbing her carry-on. "Evening flights are perfect. I get some reading done, then I sleep through most of the flight—by the time I wake up, I'm landing."

"Come on, let's have a final cup of tea before you head out." I pour the tea and we sit together, two sisters with cats on our laps, watching the quiet hum of the morning.

"France feels real now," she says, almost to herself.

"It is real," I whisper back. "And you're ready."

She doesn't answer right away—just lets out a breath and nods. I give her hand a gentle squeeze, and we sit there like that for a while—two girls with tea, and a future full of unknowns. For Destiny, it was even more complicated. Mom had a different hold on her, one that made leaving the house feel like an act of rebellion. Given how we grew up with our mother, I think we both have pinch-me moments like this. Moments where things feel too gentle, too safe, too steady to be real. But they are. We're here. And we're okay. And somehow, in that moment, it all feels okay.

*

The quiet afternoon lingers after Destiny leaves in her uber, the hum of the house settling around me. I make another cup of tea, letting the warmth soak in as I get some laundry done. My phone buzzes on the floor beside me —a text from someone I didn't expect.

*Dad: Hey Mia, I need those chairs I let you borrow awhile back. Mom wants them for a get-together we're having.*

*Me: Sure! You can meet me at the shop. I'll have them ready for you later this afternoon before we close.*

*Dad: Thanks. I'll be there at closing.*

I stare at the message, thumb hovering over the screen. Meeting Dad always feels...off. Sometimes it's like he's a stranger who's never really grown to know me. Even though we don't live far apart, he looks at me like I'm still the teenage girl he can't quite wrap his head around. Other times, it's like he's constantly weighing me, measuring me against the kid I used to be.

I let out sigh, typing a quick reply:

*Me: Anytime.*

I set the phone down and lean back against the couch, letting the thought settle. I keep the peace when I see him, stay calm, and hope that maybe one day, things will feel different—that we can be closer, not just by proximity, but by choice, by understanding, by time shared. The truth is, I look at our videos of good memories from time to time and miss it. I stand, stretching lightly, and grab my keys, load the two chairs into the trunk of my car and make my way to the shop.

"Hi, José!" I call out.

"Hey, boo! I already got the inventory shipment for the teas. Set them aside for you behind the counter," he says.

"Thanks, love! I appreciate you! I'm going to sort that out before we close" I reply.

"By the way, girl, I seen yo' man coming out the gym! That beautiful, tatted dragon—whew!" I immediately crack up.

"JOSE!!" I yell, covering my face. He fans himself dramatically.

"Don't you José me, I almost dropped my smoothie! You better keep that man hydrated, chile."

"Stop!" I laugh. "You are so messy." He gives me a look.

"Messy? I'm just speaking facts. And don't worry—I ain't say a word to him. Just admired from afar," he adds, tongue-in-cheek.

"Mmhmm. Sure—all scientific observations, right?" José strikes a dramatic pose.

"Exactly. Y'all know I'm a part-time scientist." I shake my head, laughing.

"Of course, José!" We share another laugh before I head to the back, still smiling.

I get to work, moving through the tasks. After some time passes, José clocks out, and I flip the sign to 'Closed.' I move through the shop, checking inventory, dusting off corners, straightening displays. The routine keeps my mind occupied. Then, a faint knock at the door. It's Dad. I wave him in and mouth, "It's open."

"Hey, Daddy," I say, setting down what I'm holding and turning my back to grab the chairs.

"Hey baby, how are you?" He says, voice low, controlled but still carrying some tenderness.

"I'm doing alright. Things are great. How about you?" I respond.

"Good, good," he replies, pausing for a moment. "Just getting stuff ready for—"

"For what?" I ask.

"Angie's graduating," he says finally. "We're going to her graduation to watch her walk across the stage and then throwing a party for her."

The hairs on the back of my neck stand up, a gulp rising in my throat that I immediately swallow. I'd forgotten that she was finally finishing her bachelor's. Dad had missed all of my graduations, and though it's not the time or place, I can't help but feel the familiar sting. He and my stepmom threw me a small party to resolve the absence, which was sweet. Despite the effort though, after all of their negative talk about me "never making it through school" or "being impossible", actually earning my degree only made his absence louder. Him not being there to watch me walk across the stage for high school, my Bachelors or Masters degree—wasn't something that could be replaced with cake. He'd say money was tight and couldn't afford a flight to Florida. That didn't hold weight because he made the time to fly to Florida for his cruise vacations. When I earned my master's, my stepsister Angie seemed taken aback. She said something like, 'I thought I held the highest degree in the family,' then teased, 'So, Mia, how many times are you going to graduate?' I shake my head and cancel my thoughts quickly, nearly forgetting to respond.

"Oh, that's lovely—what a tremendous accomplishment. I hope it's a great time," I say.

"Yeah," he says, pausing to look down at his phone briefly, then back at me. "Would you like to come? It's tomorrow afternoon," he adds.

For some reason, his invitation doesn't sound entirely persuasive. As much as he's asking, it feels like a formality. And honestly, I'm not sure I'm up for an awkward hangout with Angie. Something's always off with her, whether it's competition or something else. I would love to celebrate her and her accomplishments, but we just don't have that kind of relationship.

So, I lie.

"Thank you for inviting me. I actually have to drop Destiny at the airport tomorrow. She's leaving for France and with LAX traffic we have to leave early."

He never talks to Destiny, and though they have each other on social media, Destiny never posts in real time so there's no way he can fact-check that she left already.

Without hesitation, he says, "Okay, that's too bad. But that's wonderful that she's going to France."

We move the chairs together then, lifting them into the bed of his truck. The rhythm is simple, familiar, if a little stiff, like two people navigating around old habits.

"Hey," he says as we finish, brushing his hands off. "We should grab coffee sometime... catch up. I know you're busy with the shop and everything, but—" I nod, offering a small, genuine smile.

"Yeah, we should. I'd like that." He pauses almost as if he's surprised by my answer.

"Oh...okay. Nice. I'd like that, too. Or we can grab lunch or something—more time." I step back, still smiling politely.

"That sounds good. Let me know, and I'll be there." He waves, climbing into the driver's seat.

"Take care, Mia. I love you, baby."

"You too, Dad. Love you." I reply, closing the door behind me.

At last, the store feels calm again. I exhale, letting myself process. Some days, peace is just being able to stand in the quiet, even after an awkward conversation, and feel yourself ease back into equilibrium again.

# CHAPTER TWELVE
## *Khalid*

I head down to the backyard, where all the weight equipment is, hoping to get in a quick morning workout. The air is humid, still waking up—just like me. I'm still on West Coast time, but I'm managing. Then I hear a knock. I ignore it at first, thinking it's probably for my mom. But then—

"Khalid!" my mom calls from inside.

"Yeah?" I shout back, still mid-set. She doesn't answer.

"Yes, Mom?" I try again, more alert now.

"Come here," she says. Something in her voice tightens my chest. Not panicked—just...off.

I drop the dumbbell and jog inside. She's standing at the front door, looking over her shoulder at me with a face I've only seen a few times—concerned, caught in the middle. And then I see why: *Sharie.* Standing there, like we never ended. She acts as though she belongs here.

"Hi, Khalid," she says brightly, like we're good. "I tried texting, but for some reason my messages aren't going through." I stare at her.

"Hey, Sharie," I say dryly.

*Of course the messages aren't going through, I think. I blocked you. How the hell did you even know I was in Florida?*

She shifts her eyes past my shoulder.

"So can I come in, or...?" My mom hesitates, then gently steps aside.

"Sure, of course." Her voice is polite but uneasy.

My mom has always been an angel—always gracious, even to people who don't deserve it. And after whatever story Sharie spun the other day, I can't even blame her for being unsure. Sharie steps inside as if this is normal. My mom disappears down the hallway, giving us space.

"What's going on Sharie?" I say and her face fills with fury.

"What's going on?? Were you really not gonna see me after flying here?" she says in a low stern voice.

"I had to find out through Instagram? Like, are you for real right now, Khalid?!"

That's it. That's how she found out—through the story post I made when I landed. Homebound. One word. That one damn caption gave me away. I didn't block her on my social media. I study her for a moment, jaw tense.

"Follow me to the backyard, Sharie." She steps outside after me, and before I can say a word, the verbal assault begins.

"So you wanna tell me about this new bitch you're seeing in Cali?" she shoots the question at me. I look at her, caught off guard all over again, and before I can respond she doubles down as if she'd caught me in a lie. "Yeah! I saw that damn story post! and you fuck around and block me! How could you do this to me, Khalid? To us? I—"

"Us? We are not a thing anymore!" My tone spikes before I can stop it. I take a deep breath, glance away to collect myself, then meet her eyes again. "Sharie, I am done. I ended things with you months ago. And you need to watch your mouth when it comes to the woman I'm dating."

"Excuse me?" she snaps, raising her eyebrows. "Who the fuck you think you talking to?! After everything I've done for you? I don't have to watch *shit,* I—"

"Enough Sharie!" My voice is louder now and filled with annoyance. "See that's your problem, you keep pushing control as 'care'. You didn't do anything for me but box me in! You robbed me of my peace—of my time to grieve my grandfather. You made it all about you."

"Controlling?? You shut me out!" She fires back. "Like I didn't hold you down through everything!" I step back, jaw tight.

"You held me down by keeping me under. That's not love, it never was, and I won't make that mistake again." Her eyes narrow and she folds her arms.

"Wooooow...So now our relationship was a mistake?! Why do you need to talk to another bitch so badly, anyway?!"

"It's not about that, and never was. You had a problem with everyone. Even my cousins. I couldn't have a conversation with anyone without it becoming an issue. You questioned everything—who I talked to, where I went. You embarrassed me in front of my friends. Remember the time you kicked the steering wheel while I was driving because I took a wrong exit?! You did that shit in front of our friends sitting in the car with us! I couldn't breathe without you telling me how to!" She blinks. A second of stillness. "You wanted me isolated. So I'd only have you to lean on." That one hit. Her eyes flicker and grow wide. Her arms fold tighter.

"You're making the biggest mistake of your life walking away from me. And this temporary bitch? She doesn't know you like I do. We have history." I shake my head in amusement.

"I'm done arguing with you," I say then pause, while taking a step closer to her and looking her in the eyes before continuing. My voice drops, steady and final.

"And that's the last time you disrespect me and the woman I'm with. Get the fuck out my house Sharie—don't come back here again."

She gasps and her mouth drops but no words come out. The silence is thick, with pulsing tension in the space between us. Her eyes gloss over with tears, but my composure doesn't break. She takes a deep breath.

"What does she have over me, Khalid?" Her voice cracks as tears fall. "I want you back. I know I've made mistakes. I'm not perfect. Don't you have any love left for me? For us? You can't possibly be throwing away what we've had together?"

She reaches for me—arms out like she's about to pull me into something I've already escaped. I gently step back, just out of reach.

"I hope you get the healing you need," I say, "But that healing won't come from me."

Her face hardens, she blinks a few times and stares at me in shock. More tears fall and she wipes them quickly but my expression doesn't falter. After a moment more of silence, she takes a step back, turns around and heads to the sliding door. I hear her sobbing getting louder, but I turn and head back to the weights. Back to the air, to the sweat, to the ground that holds me.

*She came looking for something in me that doesn't live here anymore.*

*

"You heading out, bro?" Hakeem asks, leaning against the doorway. "If I didn't have this appointment, I'd go with you. You sure you don't wanna wait 'til I get back?"

"Nah, it's straight, man." I pull my T-shirt over my head. "I think I need to go alone anyway."

He nods slowly, reading more than I say.

"Alright. I've been running the engine on your car every couple of weeks while you were gone—just so the battery wouldn't die. Here are the keys."

He tosses them my way, and I catch them.

"Appreciate you, man." I mumble.

I slide into the driver's seat of my Impala for the first time in months. It smells like dust and something older—like the memory of me still lingers in the fabric. I sold my bike before I left; the impala I held on to. After all, my grandfather helped me with the down payment as a gift for graduating from nursing school. It's been sitting here, untouched, just like everything else I put on hold when I left Florida for California. I ease out of the driveway and onto the street, headed toward the cemetery. The route is familiar, but I feel disconnected—like I'm watching myself drive through someone else's memories.

Muscle memory knows the turns, but somehow I don't feel like I'm in my own body. I feel like a stranger driving through a version of my past. At the stoplight, I think about turning around. Maybe I'm not ready for this. Maybe I never will be. But before I can decide, the light turns green—and my foot hits the gas without thinking. It's like my body finally just decided what my mind couldn't.

*

*"The cancer is aggressive, son."*
That's what my mom said on the phone eleven months ago. Language failed me in the moment as I tried to find the words to reply. Her voice was sharp. She's normally bubbly and vibrant. I could hear quiet sobs, just enough for me to hear everything she wasn't saying. Her pain shattered me. It's hard to describe, but when you can hear that your mom isn't okay through her silence, it breaks you. I didn't allow myself to shed any tears. I felt like I wasn't allowed to break. Like I had to be strong for her even though she didn't ask me to.

We went to visit Grandpa soon after. All of us—my parents, siblings—filled the hospital room as best we could. Grandpa's wish was that we stay strong for him, and we did everything we could to honor that. Even as we lost a little more of him each day, we held on to what mattered: his spirit, his humor, the way his face still lit up when we told old stories he'd heard a hundred times. Most times he'd laugh, and it would turn into a cough. But he still smiled, and when he had the strength, he would make a joke, reminding us of how quick and witty he is. We were present in the way he asked us to be. We didn't grieve in front of him to maintain his wish. It was as though we made a pact to honor the experience he requested of us. We showed up every day, to spend every moment we could with him. Sometimes we brought food, he barely touched it though. Sometimes, he'd look at one of us with that gleam in his eye, like he knew we were doing our best to carry the weight he couldn't anymore.

Then the day came. We got the call—it was time to say goodbye.

When I got to the hospital, I was the last to arrive. They handed me a little card. It had a number to dial and a patient code. I remember gripping it like it meant something more, like it might unlock a better ending. The waiting room was empty. No nurses at the front desk. Not a single person sitting in the rows of chairs. The whole place felt like it was holding its breath. I walked to the phone in the middle of the room. My footsteps echoed against the tiled hospital floor, as if the building wanted to remind me I was alone. That, combined with the loud hum of silence and fluorescent lighting, made me feel like I was in a dream. Well, nightmare, for that matter.

I picked up the receiver, hand shaking, and dialed.

"Hi, what's your name and what patient are you calling for?" the voice on the other end asked.

"Um—Khalid. I'm here for my grandfather...Cedric."

"Okay, a nurse will meet you at the doors to the operating room to bring you to him."

When the nurse opened the door and led me back, the hallway felt endless. Every step toward the room pressed on my chest like a weight. But when I walked in and saw him—frail, quiet, breathing shallowly. Even now, his presence still carried peace.

The room was warm and dim. Mom was already at his side, holding his hand, eyes red but steady. My dad stood just behind her, a hand on her shoulder. My siblings were on the other side of the bed— Ariana had tears silently slipping down her cheeks, and Elijah just kept nodding to himself like he was trying to stay strong and eventually stepped out of the room to collect himself for a few moments before returning. Hakeem caught my eyes and gave me the smallest nod, like he knew exactly what I was feeling. Our family members lined the wall and whispered prayers that filled the air. No one was ready. No one ever is. But somehow, we were all doing our best to be strong, just like Grandpa asked. He couldn't speak anymore, but when I reached down and held his other hand, his eyes fluttered open for a moment. Just a second. Enough for me to know that he knew I was there. I bent down and whispered, "It's okay, Grandpa. You don't have to fight anymore. We love you. We thank you."

A tear falls from his eye. I gently wiped it with the edge of the sleeve of my hoodie.

One by one, we each leaned in, kissed his forehead, his hand, whispered our I-love-you's, our thank-you's, and our prayers.

*

I shut the car door and stand still for a moment, staring out at the cemetery. The air is quiet in that heavy way only graveyards seem to hold. I make my way forward slowly. By the time I reach his stone, the tears are already tugging at me. I lower myself to the ground and just sit there

for a while, letting the moment swallow me. Then I let go. I free myself—finally. My chest loosens, the tears fall, and I don't stop them this time. "I miss you so much, Grandpa," I whisper. "Every single day." My voice cracks, but I keep talking—like he's still here, like he's sitting across from me the way he used to. "What I would give to hear the warmth in your voice. I wish we had more time. I know you're still with me—I feel you, I do. I just...I miss our conversations. I miss the way you listened. The way you always knew when to speak, and when to let the silence speak instead." I brush a hand over my face. "Thank you. For everything you taught me. For the love you showed me. The care and happiness you brought me. The example you led by. You always gave me space to figure things out—even when you already knew the outcome."

I pause for a moment.

"I finally cut off Sharie. You were right about her. You saw things I couldn't—or maybe didn't want to. But you let me learn in my time, and I appreciate that more than you'll ever know." I smile a little, despite my tears. "California's been good to me. I'm staying focused. Growing. Learning how to be better. I'm saving money and eating right. I should have enough to buy my own place at the end of the contract." I pause and wipe my tears. "I swear, they don't make oxtail like they do out here. Not even close." I laugh through the ache in my chest. "Mom's cooking again. For a while, when you left, she wasn't herself. But when I came home, I saw her smile that I haven't seen since you transitioned." The wind blows the trees. I put my hand over my head to make sure my hat is on snug. "And I wanted to tell you...I met someone. Her name is Mia." A pause. "I think I'm falling in love with her, Grandpa." The words hang in the air—bare, full and real. I let them settle between us like a blessing. "I wish you could meet her. She's different. She's so genuine, she sometimes reminds me of Ma." I pause. "But it's complicated. My contract is ending. She owns her own business in California, so she can't just pick up and leave it. I don't know what the future holds for us. Part of me wants to take a chance and give this a shot even though it would change my life, moving across the country. It just feels so soon to decide. I wish I knew the path ahead of me, if I should follow this through. I wish I could talk to you about this. I wish you were here with me."

The rain falls beings to fall lightly. I glance up at the stone. A hummingbird land on it. The same hummingbirds that would constantly flock in his backyard. He's here, I just know it. I open my hands and let the raindrops collect in my palms.

Confirmation.

"Message received. I love you, Grandpa."

# CHAPTER THIRTEEN
## *Khalid*

Myself, Hakeem and my boy Dre from highschool meet up at Top Gulf to hang out for my last night before I head back to California tomorrow. The clink of golf balls and the low rumble of trendy music hum around us as I line up my shot. I swing—decent enough to shut Hakeem up for a minute, but not good enough to beat Dre's last one.

"Man, you still swing like a backup dancer," Hakeem says, slapping my shoulder.

"Keep talkin', old man. I'm warming up," I shoot back, smirking as Dre laughs behind us.

Dre's sipping his beer, watching the next guy take a swing. He's got that calm glow about him lately—probably cause he just hit seven years married and has a newborn at home.

"Hey, congratulations again, man. Little man sleeping through the night yet?" I ask. He snorts.

"Hell no. Tasha lets me think I'm helping, but really, she just wants me out of her way." He grins. "Worth it though. He's got my forehead and her attitude—pray for me." We all laugh, and I nudge Hakeem's arm.

"Hey, how's Ma been, for real since I've been gone the last few months? Hakeem shrugs, more subdued now.

"She's doing alright. Some days still hit her hard. You know how she is—she'll never say it outright, but you can tell. Lately she's been busying herself with the house. For a while there, she did little at all. Hardly cooked. Kinda just...sat with her grief." He glances at me, then smiles faintly.

"But this week, knowing you were coming home? It lifted her spirit. You saw her—she's happy to have you back, even if just for a few days."

I nod, that ache in my chest spreading a little.

"Yeah. I know. I just feel guilty not being around."

Dre looks between us, then claps my shoulder.

"You know she loves you man. And she's proud of you for getting out there and doing your thing. Between all that, you still show up and call. That's what matters."

He sips his beer, squinting.

"So, back to this West Coast girl...What's stopping you from making it permanent?" I take a slow sip.

"Man, it feels tricky. We started this knowing I'm on a contract. I don't think either of us knew where this was going. I never expected to feel this way about her, and I don't know if she feels as strongly as I do. Not to mention, it's only been a few months—I don't want her to feel pressured by me." I pause, I already know the answer. *I think I really am falling for her.* Hakeem leans back.

"I hear you on the pressure, but I want to tell you— as much as I want us to stay close, you gotta do what makes your heart right. If that means moving to California? Man, I'm with it. I don't know Mia yet, but the way you light up talking about her? She's family already."

"Yeah," I say, swirling my drink. "I know I need to decide. Time is moving fast, and I just...I want her to be comfortable. Me moving my whole life to be there? That's big—not just for me, but for her too." Dre nods.

"I hear you, bro. Trust yourself though. I think you already know what you want. And you'll never know what she's thinking unless y'all talk. Take a little more time to sort it out—I get it's still sort of soon—but don't wait until the last minute either. You're more than halfway through your contract. That time will creep up fast."

"I appreciate y'all." I say looking at both of them. Dre raises his glass.

"To Mia...and to you not dragging your feet." I grin despite myself as we clink glasses.

I step outside for a second, needing air—or maybe just needing her. The Florida night hums heavy around me, cicadas buzzing somewhere in the dark. It makes me miss her more than I want to admit. My mind begins to race with the conversation the boys and I where having. Could I move to California? Could I see myself living there permanently— for a relationship? Everything I've ever known is here in South Florida. Same palm trees, but different cities for sure.

I scroll straight to her name. FaceTime, not text. I need to see her face.

She answers on the third ring, hair a sleepy halo around her head, blanket pulled up under her chin.

"Hey, handsome," she murmurs, voice all low and honey-slow.

"Hey, pretty girl." I lean on the railing, grinning like a fool. "Did I wake you?" She shakes her head, eyes blinking heavily.

"Maybe. But it's you, so...I don't mind." I laugh quietly, thumb tracing circles over the screen like she can feel it.

"I'm with Hakeem and Dre tonight at Topgolf. We got to talking about—" I pause. The words line up behind my teeth: *How I could just come out there for good. How you're already family to them.* But I swallow it down. It's too big, too raw, too soon to say out loud. Especially through a phone. Even though I think I know what I want.

"Talking about old times," I lie, voice easy. "Stupid high school stuff." She looks amused.

"Sounds fun. Did you win?"

"Always," I wink, and she laughs through the sleep clinging to her. I take her in a little longer, committing her to memory.

"Miss you, Mia."

"Miss you more, Khalid." Neither of us says goodbye. We just stay there, quiet breathing on both ends of the line, like maybe if we're silent enough, the miles won't matter so much. Her eyes flutter shut once, twice, and I know she's drifting.

"Go to sleep, pretty girl," I whisper.

"Mmm...night, Khalid," she mumbles, voice barely there. I watch her for another moment, memorizing the way she always curls a hand under her cheek like she's guarding her own heart.

When the screen goes dark, I check my messages and see a voicemail from my recruiter.

*"Hey Khalid, it's John. I know you're contract has less than half way to go. I've been looking into other contracts to line up for you and there appears to be a lot of opportunities in New York. I know you're from the east coast, let me know if that's something you'd be interested in. The hospital is in need so it should be a shoe in..."*

I pocket my phone once the voicemail ends and let out a breath I didn't know I'd been holding. I push the door back open and find Dre and Hakeem wrapping up with the server. Dre slides his card across the table before Hakeem can argue.

"Too slow, bro," Dre says, grinning. Hakeem shakes his head.

"Whatever. Next round's on me." Dre turns to me, pulling me in for a quick hug and a solid dap.

"Proud of you, man. For real. Go get what you want. Don't drag your feet." I laugh, squeezing his shoulder.

"Look at you, giving speeches. Nah, I'm proud of you. Being a father, doing your thing —it's amazing to see, Dre. You're built for it." Dre chuckles.

"Appreciate that man. Get cuffed up already so you can have one too."

"Bet." I laugh as though it were that easy.

We say our goodbyes in the parking lot, dap and hugs and the promise to do it again sooner than we probably will. Dre heads for his truck, waving once before pulling off toward his wife and his baby boy waiting at home. Hakeem jerks his chin at me.

"You ready?"

"Yeah."

We climb into his car, the night closing around us.

*

The next morning, Hakeem and my mom drop me at the airport. She hugs me tight, then pulls back to look me over like she used to before the first day of school.

"Be safe, son," she says softly. Then, with a little smirk, she adds, "Why do I feel like you're not coming back so soon?" I laugh, but it sticks somewhere in my throat.

"Ma, I'll be back to see you. Don't start." She pats my cheek, eyes shining but playful.

"Mhm. We'll see. I love you baby. You make us all so proud."

"Thank you, love you too, Ma." Hakeem grabs my bag before I can, shaking his head smiling.

"Don't let her guilt you into a round-trip ticket." I roll my eyes, hugging him quickly before turning toward security. I don't look back right away, but I feel them both there, watching, holding me up in their own ways.

On the plane, I tuck in my headphones, Mia's sleepy face from last night still glowing in my memory. I've had an amazing time with my family, but I can't lie, I can't wait to get back to babygirl.

# CHAPTER FOURTEEN
## *Mia*

I double-check the arrival time for the fifth time, even though he texted me, "Just landed, baby. Walking out to arrivals" fifteen minutes ago. My heart's been thumping, doing the most since.

I park, check my lip gloss in the mirror, wipe it off and reapply because of course I do. Then I check it again. By the time he walks out of the terminal, dragging his carry-on behind him like he owns the whole damn airport, I'm half tempted to run up and jump on him. But I don't. I lean against my car instead, pretending to scroll my phone while my whole body buzzes at the sight of him. His eyes find me instantly.

"Hey, beautiful girl," he says, dropping his bag and pulling me in like he's been gone a year. He smells like expensive cologne.

"You're back," I mumble into his neck, trying not to look too gone for him.

"Yeah." He pulls back just enough to kiss me once, twice, like he can't help himself. "Missed you."

"Missed you more," I say, half-smiling against his mouth.

We break apart just long enough for him to toss his bag in the trunk.

He opens the passenger door for me—but when I slide in, he shuts it and strolls right around to the driver's side like its nothing. I laugh as he climbs behind the wheel.

"You're stealing my car now?" He adjusts the seat back for his legs, shooting me a smug look.

"Nah, just driving my girl home. Let me take care of you for a second." I roll my eyes, cheeks hurting from grinning.

"I can be a passenger princess." He leans over, kisses my cheek once more for good measure, then pulls us out of the lot, one hand already drifting to my thigh like he never wants to stop touching me.

"So, it's still early. I know I want to spend the rest of today with you, what would you like to do?" he asks.

"Want to catch a movie tonight? Maybe after resting and a shower?"

"Oh yeah! Let's do that!"

My smile is so wide, I don't even try to hide my excitement.

*

I sit cross-legged on the bed, laptop perched on my thighs, scrolling through Sinners showtimes like I'm planning a hostage rescue.

"6:45 or 7:15..." I mutter to myself, glancing at the bathroom door every few seconds. The shower's still running. My brain pretends to care about seats, but all I can think about is him—wet and warm and here again. I hear the water shut off.

"Khalid? Do you want—"

The bathroom door swings open, and every letter of every word I was about to say slides right out of my head.

He steps out, steam curling around him, a towel hanging low on his hips, droplets tracing the sharp lines of his abs and disappearing into that dangerous V that makes my breath stutter every time.

"You were saying?" he teases, smirk lazy, eyes locked on me like he knows exactly what he's doing.

I snap the laptop shut because…*What movie?*

"You don't play fair at all," I whisper, but it comes out half laughter. He crosses the room slowly, deliberately, stopping right in front of me. My head tips back just to keep his eyes. He leans down, nose brushing mine, his closeness settling against my lips.

"Missed you," he murmurs, voice thick, his skin still dripping.

"Khalid…" I start to say something—anything—but the second his mouth crashes into mine, everything logical dissolves.

He kisses me and I grab the edge of his towel without thinking, tugging him closer until he's right between my knees. His hands slide under my shirt, thumbs brushing the soft curve beneath my bra.

"We're not gonna make this movie," I breathe out between kisses, half a laugh, half a moan.

"Tell me to stop then," he growls against my throat, lips trailing lower as his hand gently lift my shirt up.

"Don't," I whisper. It's barely a sound, but he hears it—feels it—and that's all it takes.

He lifts his head just enough to look at me, eyes dark and hungry and mine. He pushes into me right there on my bed—my gasp swallowed by his mouth; the laptop forgotten on the floor. A rush of heat as he deepens in me, a breath caught in my throat, and suddenly I'm holding on to him, lost in the rhythm we've created.  I rise upright to sit on him so I can ride him. My head tips back, a slow breath slipping out of me as I move on him. Khalid's hands follow the curve of my spine, sending a shiver straight through me. And the moment his fingers press into my lower back, I melt forward with my chest against his and he pulls me tighter. I keep riding him, feeling my wetness gliding along on his dick as I move up and down, wanting more and more. He grips my ass with one hand, and his other hand gently holds my neck. The sensation consumes me, I feel held and stretched into something that feels impossibly good, like my soul is being fed what it's been craving. I cling to him more, closing my eyes, biting his shoulder, because I don't want to lose this feeling. His breath grazes my collarbone, and my whole body reacts before my mind can catch up. I feel my pulse rising and my body tightening as it chases this fullness. Without a word, he murmurs against my ear, "Not yet," and I obey. He holds me like he's memorizing me, like he wants every inch of closeness he can get. And the way I lean into him...I want it too. More than I can say. The way he knows my body turns me on in more ways than one. Then, finally, with a low, commanding whisper, he says, "Now, baby."

I can't help myself—without thinking, I pick up speed and scream his name as he brings me orgasm. I lay forward on him gasping for air. We stay like that for a moment—me still catching my breath, his forehead resting against mine, both of us just listening to the quiet between us. His thumb drifts over my hip in drawing circles. I slide my fingers through the damp small coils at his nape, tracing the edge of his hairline until he lets out a soft laugh against my cheek.

"You good?" he murmurs, voice low and hoarse in a way that makes me want him all over again.

"Yeah," I whisper, smiling because it's true. "You?" He leans back just enough to look at me, eyes soft, grin lazy.

"Better than good." His gaze flicks to the laptop still half-open on the floor. "Think we've still got time to make *Sinners?*" I let out a laugh— for real this time—and bury my face in his shoulder.

"I'm not about to play with you. We're late, Khalid."

"I want popcorn. And I wanna sit next to my girl in the back row like a teenager and watch her pretend she's not about to fall asleep on me." I roll my eyes, shoving at his shoulder playfully.

"Fine. Shower again and get dressed. And this time, keep the towel on until you have clothes ready, please. I'll shower afterwards to avoid any other distractions happening."

He chuckles, leaning in to steal one more kiss before standing naked and unbothered to scoop up the abandoned towel.

"Yes, ma'am." He disappears back into my bathroom, I collapse back against on my bed, grinning up at the ceiling.

Late or not, we're making that movie after we just made a movie.

*

"Man. *Sinners* was great, but I thought the ending would be different," he says, one hand draped lazily over the wheel as we cruise down the quiet streets back to my place. His other hand finds a mine on the console..

"I loved everything about it, especially the music! I'm glad we saw it. It feels like everyone's been talking about it," I say, giving his hand a playful squeeze when he bumps my knuckles at a red light.

"It was real good, shit worth it for the popcorn alone. You didn't even finish yours, by the way."

"Because you ate it before I could!" I shoot back, rolling my eyes. "Greedy."

"Aye, we suppose to be kind to one another!" He laughs, quoting Cornbread from the movie and I crack up. A few streetlights pass before I shift in my seat, curiosity tugging at me. "Hey—off topic, but...tell me about your trip. How was it? Seeing your family again?" His thumb drifts over my knuckles, tracing lazy circles.

"It was good," he says, sounding a little more settled now. "Real good, actually. The siblings and cousins were on their usual bullshit—talking shit, playing cards 'til stupid hours, ganging up on me whenever they could. We caught up on everything, laughed too much. Felt like being a kid again for a second." He pauses, and I watch the faint smile flicker brighter when he mentions her. "Ma's good too. Better than I expected. She's been keeping herself busy—probably too busy, but that's how she is. She was really excited to see me. I could tell she needed that." His grip on my hand tightens a bit before he relaxes again, glancing sideways at me with a gentleness that makes my heart tug.

"I'm glad you went, love," I say. "You look refreshed. I'm glad you had that time with them."

For a split second, my mind drifts to the time he has left on his contract. Roughly two months left. The words catch at the edge of my tongue—*What happens now?* And—*How are you feeling about us?* It

106

bubbles up, but I swallow it back before it reaches my lips. Not tonight. Tonight is easy. Tonight doesn't need those questions. I clear my throat and squeeze his hand once.

"Did you...did you visit your grandpa while you were there?" He looks at me with vulnerability in his eyes, like he knows exactly what I didn't ask but answers the one I did, anyway.

"Yeah. I did," he says, voice quiet but steady. "Sat out there for a bit. Talked to him. Felt good, honestly." He pauses, thumb brushing over my knuckles. "It was my first time visiting his grave. I didn't think I could do it. But when I did...it felt like he was right there with me." I nod, pressing my thumb into the back of his hand, holding that moment with him without needing to fill it with anything else. Outside, the city slides by in hushed pools of streetlight and quiet houses. Before I know it, we're pulling up to my place. His motorcycle is still parked out front from our date before he left for Florida. He cuts the engine, lets our hands linger a moment longer, then gets out and comes around to open my door.

"You don't have to walk me up," I tease as he pulls me close, his bag slung over one shoulder.

"Yeah, I do," he murmurs, lips brushing my hair as we climb the steps.

At my door, we pause under the porch light. He sets his bag down just long enough to cup my face with one hand, his thumb tracing my jaw like he's memorizing it all over again.

"Thanks for tonight," he says. "For everything."

"You don't have to thank me," I whisper, leaning into his touch. "Just get some sleep tonight, please."

His expression eases as he dips his head and kisses me—slow and gentle, the kind of kiss that says there's more waiting for us than either of us knows how to name yet. When he pulls back, I swear there's something else in his eyes—something he wants to say but tucks away for another time.

"Okay," I breathe, trying not to hold on to his hoodie when he lets go.

He grabs his bag again, and heads to his bike, snaps his helmet into place, and glances up at me one more time—with that grin I'll never be strong enough to resist. He revs the engine, two rumbles then pulls away slow into the night. I watch him until his bike disappears, then I slip inside my door, heart full and quiet, and lock the night behind me.

Some questions can wait. Tonight, this was enough.

# CHAPTER FIFTEEN
## *Khalid*

It's been a few weeks since I've been back at work after Florida, but it's my first shift running into James, our schedules have been opposite of each other as of late. The time change had me sideways at first, but I'm back to sleeping right, and hitting the gym after these twelve hour long shifts. I've seen Mia a few times in between—whenever she's not picking up extra hours at the shop while her sister's off living her best life in France. Mia told me her stay has extended, and as a result I've been between my Airbnb and her place, playing house and staying over whenever our availability allows it. Just enough time with her to feed my soul mentally and spiritually. I'd be lying if I said I didn't enjoy playing house with her over the last few weeks.

"Welcome back, man! It's good to see you—how was Florida?" James, daps me up as I walk into the break area.

"It was great, man," I say, setting down my bag. "Great to see family again. I'm glad I went."

"That's what's up," James nods. "You don't have much longer in your contract, do you? About a month left?"

"Yeah, man—nearly five months went by in a blink."

"Damn, it's flying by." He smirks. "Unless you're trying to live here! You know they're opening up some permanent positions in the next couple of weeks. Management loves your work ethic—hell, everybody does." I let out a breath and shake my head.

"I haven't really thought about that yet. I mean, it was supposed to be temporary. My Airbnb, everything—it's all short term. I'm supposed to go to New York next. I think that's where my recruiter's looking."

"For real?" James raises an eyebrow. "What about shorty?" He offers a teasing look now. "The one with the big curly hair?" As soon as he says it, I catch movement out of the corner of my eye. Sierra walks by, close enough to hear, though pretending not to be. She avoids eye contact; her face is unreadable. Ever since I turned her down gently, she hasn't said much. Still, she always seems to be wherever I am. I glance at James, giving him a look that says, wait. He follows my eyes, spots Sierra, and shoots me a knowing look. Once she's out of earshot, I lower my voice.

"Man, I don't know," I admit. "It's hard to say. We haven't really talked about it much. Maybe neither of us wants to put pressure on things. Her business is here—I can't ask her to leave that. And if I stay, would it feel like I'm moving too fast? We've only been dating for roughly five months. That's not that long." James shrugs.

"I feel you. But y'all aren't twenty anymore. You're both grown, established. I wouldn't say this to everybody, but time isn't the only thing worth weighing."

"You could be right, bro." I nod.

"He grabs his bag, then pauses. "Oh—before I forget. Everyone at work is getting together again this weekend. You should pull up. And bring Mia this time. Folks been wantin' to meet the woman keeping you smiling at work." I laugh under my breath.

"Yeah, we'll see."

Before James can respond, Sierra swoops back in like she'd just happened to circle around.

"Oh yes, you should definitely come," she says, eyes cutting to me for half a second too long. "It's fun, the music is good...wear something you can move in. I make everybody dance, it's really a time." James coughs into his fist, trying not to laugh. I force a polite smile.

"I'll keep that in mind."

"Do that," she says, letting the words hang like a dare before walking off again. James widens his eyes at me once she's gone.

"Bro...good luck."

"I'm gonna need it," I mutter. He chuckles.

"I'm out, but I'll catch you later—we still owe ourselves that gym session."

I walk over to the assignment board and overhear Zach, our lead, giving a report to the night shift. Zach's soft-spoken. He really cares about the team and doesn't usually have issues with anyone. A new policy just rolled out around calling out sick, and it's his job to explain it and answer questions. I catch some tension building in his voice as Buell talks over him. Buell's a senior RN with a reputation—loud, aggressive, always ready to escalate something simple. I've heard him go at it with Zach before. Zach tries his best, but he's not the confrontational type. Their voices rise.

"Fuckin idiot! Can't even answer the simple questions I'm asking you!" Buell snaps, then walks away mid-conversation—cutting Zach off in front of everyone. Before the meeting is even over with. I stand nearby and watch. Zach quickly wraps the report and steps off to the side. His face is red, and his eyes are glossy—like he's trying to hold it together. I follow him into the office.

"Zach," I say, voice low but firm. "What the fuck was that?" He turns, startled.

"Oh—hey, Khalid." His voice cracks. I step closer.

"That was unacceptable. That guy just goes off on you in front of the whole team? Again?" Zach sighs, defeated.

"I don't know, man. That guy always gets like that, no matter what I do or say."

"Have you talked to any of the other leads? Stacey? That shit ain't cool, bro. You're our lead. He should respect you. And beyond that, nobody should be treated like that—manager or not." He shakes his head.

"I want to...I really do. But I just got this lead position. I'm supposed to hold my own, right? I can't go to Stacey..." I look him in the eye.

"Zach, how about I support you? I'll help you gather reports from others in the hospital that have had altercations with him. You're not the only one he's come at sideways. I know I've only been here a few months but I have definitely noticed it."

"You'd do that Khalid?" He asks in a hopeful voice.

"Of course. I don't play that. It makes the whole work environment uncomfortable for everybody."

"If you could do that..." He exhales. "I'd really appreciate it."

*

Later that evening, I make my rounds—careful, casual, nothing forced. I catch Asia by the medical supplies area.

"Hey, Asia, you got a second?"

"Hey Khalid! Yeah, what's up?" She responds.

"You ever have issues with Buell? I mean...how he talks to folks?" I ask, keeping my voice low. She stops what she's doing, then raises an eyebrow.

"Why? Something happen?"

"He disrespected Zach in front of everybody and I don't want it to get swept under the rug. It's been going on for a bit now. I'm putting together something—a few statements. You don't have to, but if you've experienced anything that has made you uncomfortable, I'll report it and if you'd like I can keep your name anonymous." Asia doesn't even hesitate.

"He's gone off on me twice. Once over something, he charted

wrong but blamed on me. I've said something before, but it went nowhere."

"That shit is not okay," I say seriously.

"Agreed. I'll write something up. Give me a few minutes."

Shortly after my encounter with Asia, I find Luis in the break room, washing his hands.

"Yo, can I talk to you real quick?" He grabs a paper towel, drying off.

"What's up?"

"I'm putting together anonymous reports about Buell—how he treats people, talks to staff..." Luis drops the towel in the trash.

"Yeah...I got wind of that meeting this morning. Dude's been unchecked for way too long. You doing this to support Zach?" I nod.

One by one, I collect the statements, and by the end of the shift I have enough evidence: six whole reports to support Zach. I head back to the office to meet him right before the end of our twelve-hour shift. I stack the papers on the desk. He looks at the it, skimming over the top page silently. He lets out a gigantic sigh of relief.

"Thank you, Khalid. You really had my back and I appreciate it" he says. He then grabs  the stack of papers and shuffles through them. "No need to thank me, bro." I nod.

"I really thought I was the only one dealing with this." He murmurs.

"You weren't, man. Let's make sure this place feels comfortable—for all of us."

I head out to the parking lot once my work is done and run a hand over my face without thinking about it, making my way over to my bike. Some days you fix people. Some days, you let the sweet things fix you. Tonight, I want both. Helmet in one hand, phone in the other. I unlock it, scroll straight to her name.

*Me: What are you doing, bae?*

Bubbles appear almost immediately.

*Mia: I just got home from work my love. What's up?*

*Me: Want some ice cream?*

*Mia: I would love some actually.*

*Me: What's your favorite flavor?*

*Mia: Ube*

*Me:* Bet, be at your place in 30 minutes

*Mia: Okay thank you. You're so considerate.*

I slide on my helmet and take off like I'm running late. It sounds corny, but when we have time to hang out, I don't want any minutes—or even seconds—wasted.

I pull up at her house just as the sky fades into that calm evening blue. I grab the little brown bag from the compartment under my seat, still cold from the shop, and head to her front porch. The door swings open before I can even knock. She's there—bare legs, small shorts, and a cropped tank that shows just enough skin to make it hard to look away. Her hair's wrapped in a silk scarf, a few curls peeking out around her face.

"Where's my ice cream, fool?" she teases, eyes lighting up. I smirk.

"You know I got it, pretty girl. Come here."

Before she can say another word, I wrap an arm around her waist and lift her off the floor to kiss her, while still walking us both inside, swinging the door shut with my other hand behind us. She laughs against my neck. We end up in her room, legs tangled on the bed, sharing spoonfuls from the same cup. She's got her head on my shoulder, talking between bites.

"I didn't ask you by the way, how was work today?" she asks. I shrug, taking another spoonful.

"Work was smooth. I had to step in with some work drama, but it's all handled. Other than that, a good day."

"Work drama?" she asks again.

"Yeah—some confrontation between coworkers, borderline bullying. I had to collect some statements."

"Wow, okay lead!"

"Man, chill. It's not all that serious!" I say laughing. I glance down at her, brushing my thumb over her thigh.

"When would you like to go out again?" She looks up, smiling.

"Actually, I've been craving Haitian food. Why don't I cook for you instead?" My mouth curves to a smile before I can stop it.

"I'd love to try your cooking, actually. That would be nice."

"Saturday I'm closing the shop, I might be a bit tired but would you like to come by Sunday? We can pick up groceries early that day."

"Sunday works, I have a work outing that evening, drinks and shit, I was actually going to ask you to come."

"Sure, I'm down with that." She then flips open a notebook on her nightstand. I notice the handwriting, ink still fresh.

"You been writing?" I ask.

"Yeah, just a little something," she says, glancing up at me. "Someday I'd like to write a book." I tilt my head, curious.

"What would you write about?" A small curve tugs at her lips.

"A love story, for sure. I love, love. The kind that makes you feel something deep, you know? It fills my cup emotionally reading romance."

"Yeah. I can see that. You'd make people feel it too." She laughs quietly, trying to hide a blush.

"You think so?"

"I know so." We shift a little after that. She leans in, and I meet her halfway. The kiss starts slow, then deepens, her hand finding the back of my neck. I start kissing her neck and slowly lift her shirt and rub her breasts.

"Sit on my face," I murmur. She giggles, voice low.

"Khalid, really?"

"Yeah, come on. I missed you."

She kisses me and smiles against my mouth, teasing, and it makes my pulse kick. I pull her shorts off, she climbs over my face and my hands come up to grip both her ass cheeks. All I know is her laugh, the warmth of her skin, the taste of ube ice cream, and her. Her breath slips from her mouth in a soft moan and my hands tighten at her hips pulling her closer. Her body reacts instantly as I lick her lips in her center. I motion her gently so she's riding my face. I take my time here, letting her settle into it, as the tension builds and eventually, I stick my tongue inside her. Her breathing changes, shorter, uneven until she reaches for the headboard, fingers curling it tightly.

"Baby—I—I want—" She trips over her words moaning as she climaxes, and then slowly shifts her body back to my chest to look in my eyes.

"I want you to hit it from the back," she commands. Slowly, I take off my pants while holding her gaze.

"Turn around," I murmur.

She hops off and moves with intention, brushing her skin against mine deliberately as she gets down in front of me. I look at the curvature of her spine, unclasp her bra strap and I enter her slowly. My dick was already hard but when I put it inside her, she feels even warmer than usual and her wetness dripping hits me all at once.

"Fuck, Mia," I gasp.

Her head dips, curls spilling forward as she moans, stretching her arms forward like she's surrendering. She presses back slowly into me with purpose, the bed creaks and I steady her at the waist, letting her ass recoil. We keep going, each stroke getting deeper than the last, the bed answering each motion. I feel her gripping my dick, it feels so good and it damn near knocks me off balance. I lean over her slightly so my hand slides forward from her hip finding her clit to apply light pressure as I'm thrusting. She moans loud, becomes wetter as her voice echoes the room. The reaction is instant, and enough to send a rush through me. We keep at it, I pick up speed pounding it as her moaning intensifies.

"Khalid! Fuck!"

*Perfect.*

"Come on that dick, baby," I whisper, my voice raspy and my breath staggered.

The words barely leave my mouth before her body tightens beneath me. Her fingers curl into the blankets, bunching the fabric tight as her body tenses and the moment over takes us both. She lets out a scream and I pull back to collect myself. Our heat is unmatched. A few moments pass and I head to her bathroom to grab us  both a towel.

"You good, bae?" I ask her in a low voice as I hand it to her. I look at her body spread out on the bed, her eyes still close as she catches her breath.

"I didn't know it could ever feel like this." She opens her eyes and gets off the bed to stand in front of me, grabs the towel and wraps it around her. I rest my forehead against hers for a couple moments and we stand there in silence. Not rushing past this.

I just want to please her, as though I'm making up for the lost time it took to meet her. She's got this pull I can't resist even if I wanted to. I don't just want her, I honor her.

*

Mia holds the grocery list in one hand, her phone in the other, pushing the cart with her hip. I walk alongside her, scanning the shelves.

"Alright," she says, tapping the list with her nail. "We need green plantains, scotch bonnets, vinegar, cabbage, carrots, onions, garlic...and oh, we need to get coconut milk—for Diri Kole ak Pwa or...the rice and beans."

"I see you with the bilingual flex, I got it," I reply smiling, grabbing the plantains and dropping them into the cart. "Heavy lifting is my job this afternoon." She says with a sly smile and an eyebrow raised.

"That and peeling. Don't think you're off the hook."

"I knew there was a catch." We turn down the produce aisle next, where the air smells faintly of cilantro and wet earth. Mia reaches for a bunch of green onions, inspecting them before dropping them into the cart.

"Teach me something in Creole." Her brows lift slightly in surprise.

"Oh? You trying to learn?"

"Yeah, what would I call you in Creole that's equivalent to baby?"

She doesn't hesitate. "Chérie."

"Chérie," I repeat slowly testing it out. "Yeah, I like that."

"I appreciate you trying, it's sweet." She says as we walk a few steps further with our cart.

"You ever think about growing your own stuff?" she asks, eyes scanning the rows of vegetables. "Like a little backyard garden? I want that one day—a house with a beautiful yard. I'd grow mangoes, squash, peppers, thyme...all that good stuff." I glance at her then, taking in the way her eyes soften when she talks about it.

"You'd be dangerous with a garden like that." She laughs.

"Please, I'm still learning. I'm not the best plant caretaker yet, but I'm getting there. My babies at home are training me—half of them thriving, the other half holding on for dear life." I grin at her.

"So basically, it's survival of the fittest in your townhome."

"Exactly." She bumps her hip against the cart again, smiling. "But I'll get better. I'm manifesting a green thumb and a backyard to match." We round the corner toward the fish counter. Mia leans forward, studying the fillets laid out on crushed ice like they were diamonds on display. The guy behind the counter waits patiently while she squints and tilts her head, lips pursed in concentration. Finally, she taps the glass with her nail.

"That one looks the freshest. Can I get two of those?" She points to two small snappers—a good portion size for a dinner for two, already properly cleaned and gutted.

"You gonna tell me why you're acting like Chef Ramsay right now?"

I ask.

"Because," she says, smiling as the worker wrapped up her order, "I need to make my Haitian aunties proud." I chuckle, shaking my head.

"High-stakes cooking. Got it." She angles the cart toward the peppers, sliding her eyes my way.

"Besides, it's been a long week. We deserve a proper meal before your work thing later. Drinks with your coworkers? If I'm showing up to that, I need to eat first."

"Fair enough," I say, tossing a bag of rice in the cart. "Fuel before drinks."

"Exactly, and you're not about to have me tipsy on an empty stomach. That's how poor decisions are made." I laugh as I watch her body move around the cart to grab what she needs off the shelf. Date night at home wasn't supposed to be fancy, but somehow, with her, it feels like it will be.

"Sooo…" she draws out, giving me a side-eye, "you've been working with your coworkers for a while now. Even hung out with them at the gym and stuff. I imagine they're nice?"

"Oh yeah, they're cool. I like them, James actually insisted I bring you. You'll meet him and all these other muscle heads."

"Mmm, muscle heads. Guess I'll blend right in."

Just then, my phone lights up; I'd forgotten it was still on 'Do Not Disturb.' A voicemail from my recruiter flashes across the screen. I slide the phone back into my pocket. I'll check it later, I think. I still haven't brought up the New York contract to her and definitely don't think now is the time, though I do need to tell her soon…I just need to plan things the right way, thinking through everything I'm going to say so she doesn't feel pressured but also knows my intention. The short of it is this: I would be willing to move to California for her, and I want to share my life with her.

As we reach the checkout, our cart piled high—peppers, rice, fresh snapper wrapped tight in butcher paper—she starts digging in her purse and pulling out her card. I step in front of her, gently moving her out of the way with my arm.

"Excuse meee!" she laughs, swatting at me. I shake my head, sliding my card into the reader before she can protest.

"You not paying for shit with me," I say with a smirk. "Fuck I look like?"

"Okay, I see you, provider!" She laughs again, shaking her head like I'm being dramatic. But as she packs each grocery bag, curls bouncing, eyes still bright even under the dull grocery store lights, I catch myself smiling for too long.

*Providing for you would be an honor.*

*

Once we arrive back at her townhome, we head straight into her kitchen and begin unpacking the ingredients. There's music playing low from a Bluetooth speaker in the corner of the room, old-school R&B filling the small space. Mia cutely ties on an apron then, her ass bouncing behind it as she moves.

"Alright, chef," she says, sliding over to the counter. "You're on plantain duty. I don't want to hear any complaints."

"Yes, ma'am," I say, grabbing the peeler. "If this turns out well, I'm sending a picture to my mom. She'll swear I actually know how to cook," I say. Mia looks down softly. Shit. I'd forgotten her mother had passed. "Shit...I'm sorry, baby," I say. She glances up quickly.

"Oh no! Umm, it's fine." She looks around the kitchen, searching for words, the awkwardness hanging between us for a second.

"My mother was a lot of things, good and well complicated," she begins, picking her words carefully. "But on the good days, she was kind, funny...she did so much for my sisters and me. Her and my father, though, they both have their ways but my mom in particular...she was different to me because she sacrificed so much. She came to this country, not knowing the English language, by herself, just for a better life. We didn't always get along, and I have to admit, while we had our highs...our lows were very painful." she pauses, and I listen quietly and she absorbs it.

"But, I'm still thankful. I wish I knew more about my Haitian roots. But she taught me so much. I'm grateful she taught me Creole at such a young age. I might not speak it as fast as my aunts do, but I can get by." She pauses and smiles, and I notice her eyes glossing over as if holding back tears.

"When I'm cooking with my Haitian roots, I know I'm my mother's daughter. The summer she took me there to see the land and meet the rest of our family really made an impact on my life." I reach over and gently squeeze her hand, a quiet acknowledgment passing between us. I step back slightly, watching her move around the kitchen with ease, chopping, seasoning, tasting. It's an honor to be here, in her presence, watching her put so much love and passion into this meal. And to be part of it, to share it with her...it's more than I could ask for.

I carefully slice the green plantains, dropping each piece into the hot oil as Mia moves with confidence at the stove, frying the snapper she had marinated in her homemade Epis: a fragrant mix of garlic, scotch bonnet, parsley, and lime. The kitchen fills with the sizzling symphony of oil, garlic, and the faintly sweet aroma of plantains.

"You know," Mia says, flipping a fillet expertly, "pikliz is technically better after it sits for a couple of days. All the flavors...they marry and really hit. But honestly? Fresh, right now? It still slaps." I laugh, turning a plantain in the pan.

"Listen, I am not waiting three days to try this meal either, I know you heard my stomach growling."

"Oh, I did!" she laughs. "But don't worry—mine has been singing the same tune." I begin adding the coconut milk carefully and stirring in the beans and spices. Between the creamy aroma and the sharp scent of frying plantains, I can't help but feel proud of the little symphony we've been creating together.

Once everything is cooked, we move to the counter to plate our creations. I carefully arrange the fried plantains on my plate, topping each one with a generous spoonful of pikliz, the bright colors popping against the golden plantains. Mia places her perfectly fried snapper beside a neat row of sliced bell peppers and avocado, the vibrant reds, greens, and yellows making the plate look like art. I take a deep breath and lift the lid from the pot of rice and beans. Steam rises; the beans are perfectly cooked, and the grains fluffy. *Damn, this came out perfect.* Pride swells in my chest—*We nailed it.*

"Mia, this looks incredible," I say, sliding a glass of passionfruit juice across the counter to her. She gives a humble expression, picking up her glass.

"I appreciate you kicking it with me in the kitchen." I raise my glass in a mock toast. We sit down at her small table, the colorful plates between us, steam rising and mingling with the sweet-tart scent of passionfruit. Every bite bursts with vibrant flavor, the way Caribbean culture brings it.

"GOT DAYUM!!" I yell in excitement. As I lift my hand to snap my fingers appreciatively, my mouth waters with every bite.

"It's so damn good!" she adds. "We did it!" I lean back slightly, grinning and whipping my hands with a napkin.

"Alright," I cut in abruptly, eager to throw her a curve ball, "worst date you've ever been on—go." Mia rolls her eyes, a smirk tugging at her lips.

"Oh, this happened just recently. We went to a casual place, and at the end...he straight-up asked to split the bill—after eating the French fries off my plate. Didn't even ask. Just...took them." She makes a face as if she can still taste the audacity.

"That didn't happen! He's tripping for that!" I say laughing.

"Oh, that wasn't it," she says, setting down her fork with exaggerated precision, her fingers lingering on the edge of the plate. "He tried to touch my curls—with his greasy fingers!"

"Oh, no. Buddy a menace." I shake my head, still laughing, but catch a flash of genuine indignation in her eyes. She leans back slightly in her chair.

"Okay...but what about you? Tell me more about your last serious relationship? I know we talked about it briefly at the beach."

My chest tightens. Sharie. I'd never told her about *Sharie* making her surprise visit at home or the entire ordeal. *But I should,* I think. I want to be honest. I clear my throat.

"Hmm...I..." I glance down at my plate, then back at her. "Actually, Mia, I think I should've told you sooner. I don't know why I didn't. It's not a secret or anything." She tilts her head, one eyebrow lifted, her fork resting forgotten in her hand, waiting. "I dated a woman named Sharie for two years. I ended things around the time my grandfather passed... but I allowed her to linger, up until I got here." My hands tighten slightly on the table.

"Wait, I'm a little confused...What do you mean Khalid?" Concern creeps into her voice, and she leans a fraction closer.

"My ex and I had this toxic cycle. Though we had been broken up for a few months, she was still around a lot. Not romantically but still very present, nonetheless. When I got here, I told her I was done and that I felt the separation was necessary, we didn't have a real friendship anyway. When I went back home, she found out I was in town and stopped by my mom's house unannounced." I exhale, shaking my head at the memory. "This time, I didn't leave a door open."

I observe Mia, she's not making eye contact, just quietly wipes her mouth with a napkin. Her expression turns but I can't make it out. For a moment, she seems lost in thought, lips pressing together slightly. Then, almost abruptly, she shakes her head, blinks, and gives a small smile that falters. Her eyes flick away from me, like she's weighing her words carefully.

"I see...thank you for telling me, Khalid." She pauses. "I know we're intimate, and while it matters to me we're only intimate with each other and not just out here swapping spiritual debris with multiple people, I know I can't have expectations with you being here on temporary contract." She pauses again before letting out a sigh. "You don't owe me anything." I open my mouth, wanting to respond, but before I can get a word in she adds, almost as if to save me from myself, "Anyway...we should get going. Your coworkers' event starts soon."

I feel it—a punch straight to my chest at the speed of her shift—but I try my best to hide it, forcing a laugh as I push my chair back. She, of course, doesn't miss a beat, already standing and gathering her things, like nothing heavy had passed between us at all. We carry our plates to the sink in silence. I want to be quiet for a moment, letting the sounds of running water and clinking dishes fill the space. And then the thought comes, quiet but persistent: *Was that her way of telling me she doesn't see a future with us?*

# CHAPTER SIXTEEN
## *Mia*

We head over to his motorcycle, and I slip my purse over my shoulder and helmet onto my head, trying to steady my thoughts. My chest still feels tight, a mix of curiosity and something heavier that I don't want to name aloud. He moves beside me casually, but I can feel the quiet weight between us...*We're not exactly exclusive,* I remind myself again, trying to anchor my own expectations. *But I do like him*—a lot... more than like. I shake my head almost as if to cancel the thought. I need to keep my ground, keep some clarity, or else the uncertainty might swallow me whole. I stare at the back of him for a moment as he hops on the motorcycle, wondering if he was replaying our conversation just as I was. For a fading second, I'm thankful we're riding the motorcycle, with no potential for a quiet, tense car ride where neither of us would know what to say.

I exhale slowly and fasten my helmet strap, trying to forget the weight of the kitchen conversation and yet, my thoughts linger, stubborn and persistent.

*What did he want me to say? What do we really mean to each other at this point? Did either of us really know where this was going? While I know in my heart I wish it wasn't temporary, I refuse to be the one to initiate plans for him to stay here in California—it would have to be his judgment. If he's serious, he would need to propose that. Not to mention, it couldn't be me moving either; I can't just pick up my business and leave. Not a chance. He knows that...right?* I hop on behind him, trying to push the questions away.

"Ready?" he calls out to me over the motorcycle roar.

"Yeah!" I respond. He kicks back the kickstand, and we take off. Whatever tonight is meant to hold, I won't let it unravel before we even get there.

*

We pull up to the event, and just like that, the weight of our kitchen conversation seems to evaporate. Somehow, we both slip into our roles seamlessly—friendly, confident, and as casual as if nothing happened.

"Yo! You made it!" James calls, waving as we step closer.

"What's up, man?" Khalid replies, excitement lacing his voice.

"Hi, nice to meet you." I say to James as he gives me a quick side hug.

"Pleasure, pleasure! It's good to finally meet you, you must be Mia!" James says, kindly.

More coworkers make their way over to introduce themselves and say what's up to Khalid. For a guy on a temporary contract everyone seems to gravitate towards Khalid. I'm not surprised—he's hilarious and endearing.

"Oh my gosh, girl, you're stunning!" one of his female coworkers exclaims, giving me a bright, appraising look. I laugh lightly, feeling my cheeks flush.

"Oh my gosh, thank you, love! So are you!"

I steal a quick glance at Khalid, catching the ease in his expression as he introduces me. The way he carries himself, charming and relaxed, makes it almost effortless to pretend the kitchen conversation had never happened. And for the moment, I let myself enjoy that. A few of the coworkers lean in, intrigued expressions on their faces.

"So, Mia," a coworker named Lexi asked, tilting her head, "What do you do?" A small smile tugs at my lips.

"I actually own a floral coffee shop. It's a little space downtown called Charmed—flowers, coffee, a cozy vibe. I love it."

"Oh my gosh," another coworker exclaims, eyes wide, "I've been there a few times! I am absolutely obsessed with that place! I had no idea you were the owner!" I laugh bashfully, a mix of pride and shyness coloring my cheeks.

"Well, thank you! That's so sweet of you to say. I'm glad you enjoy it—it means a lot." Lexi leans in a little closer, lowering her voice like she's sharing a secret.

"No forreal, I love the vibe there. Every time I walk in, it just makes me happy. And now, knowing you're the one behind it? I love supporting female owned businesses!" Before I say another word, Khalid rubs my back.

"What can I get you to drink, baby?" he asks, his voice low and teasing.

"Hmm...I'll have what you're having," I respond, letting myself relax a little.

"Moscow mule it is," he replies, flashing that easy smile before heading off to get our drinks.

Conversation carries on around me as he walks away, but then something catches my eye—a girl walking toward me, her friend at her side. They don't appear to be a couple, but their gaze is fixed on me, coordinated, sharp, and direct.

"Sooo...you must be Mia! It's so nice to finally meet you!"

"Oh!" I answer, slightly caught off guard. There's something about her energy that puts me on edge, though I can't put my finger on why.

"It's nice to meet you too." We shake hands but I feel her only grab the tip of my fingers "Um...I don't think I got your name?" I add after a moment of silence.

"Oh! It's Sierra—I work with Khalid all the time," she says knowingly, a small, almost teasing curve on her lips.

"Oh, cool! Well, it's nice to meet you all," I say, smiling genuinely. "I have to say, I'm in awe of all the work you do. Truly—it's not just for the weak, you all are heroes." There isn't a hint of exaggeration in my voice as I say this—I genuinely recognized RNs, RTSs—really, all medical professionals—as heroes. Lexi chimes in, grinning.

"Sierra, Mia was actually just telling us that she owns that stunning floral shop—Charmed! We've been there—remember those delicious marshmallow lattes we tried, and those soft baked chocolate chip cookies?"

"Oh!" Sierra says, her eyes widening slightly. "I had no idea! So wait...you're not a medical professional?" For a moment, I feel a flicker of condesension in her tone, though I can't tell if I'm imagining it.

"No, that's not my calling in life. I can hardly see the sight of blood." I reply, keeping my smile steady.

"Oh, okay...it's funny. Most of us medical professionals usually end up dating in the field because only we can empathize with just how intense and stressful our work is," she says, tilting her head. "But I'm sure you do a great job being there for Khalid. He raves about you a lot." I meet her gaze with a small, composed expression.

"I think empathy shows up in more ways than one." For a beat, her expression falters—but then she recovers, swirling her drink like she's debating whether to keep talking.

"That's true," she says finally, nodding. "Especially with long-distance relationships. Those definitely take a lot of empathy. It couldn't be me." My face doesn't waver, but something in my chest does.

"Long-distance?"

"Oh—" She expels air through her nose with a small chuckle, glancing toward the bar where Khalid stands talking to James. "Well, yeah. When his New York contract starts. I just assumed he told you."

For half a second, the words don't land. Then they do—all at once. A small, sharp silence fills my head. I can see Khalid just a few feet from me, laughing with Lexi, James, and the others about something trivial, completely unaware of the ripple Sierra has just caused. My mind races for a split second.

*Why didn't he tell me about this? His contract ending is just around the corner, a whole cross-country move isn't a "slipped your mind" type of detail...*I catch Sierra's gleam, that little edge in her voice, and I feel my irritation flare.

*This Heffa.*

"Oh, don't worry," she continues. "Maybe it just slipped his mind? You know, we medical professionals just tell each other everything—we're like a tight community, and work has been real busy these last few weeks...like for real, we've been in the trenches!"

The way she says real busy spikes my annoyance.

Ma'am.

"Right, well he and I will just take it one day at a time. I'm not worried." She looks at me for a moment, almost as though to resolve herself and think of a comeback.

"Oh of course, I mean a fling ain't serious anyways!" My eyes grow wide.

Alright, bet. *You want this man's dick; that much is clear.*

"Actually..." I say before I can stop myself, my tone cool but cutting, "I don't think that's any of your business."

The words slip out sharper than I had intended. I hadn't planned on arguing with one of his coworkers—but how dare she try to disrespect me? Or insinuate anything about what Khalid and I have? Sierra looks caught off guard then, her mouth opening as if to reply, but before she can get a word out, Khalid appears at my side, handing me my drink.

"Here you go, baby," he says, the familiar reassurance, grounding me. Then he glances at Sierra, his gaze sharp and steady, as if he can sense something is off. "Sierra," he says, calm but deliberate, "I see you've met Mia?"

"Actually—" I start.

"YES!" she cuts in sharply, her tone almost too eager. "She was just telling me about that little shop she owns. I had no idea—you never mentioned it, Khalid!"

"Yeah...She does." Khalid responds steadily. I take a slow sip of my Moscow mule, letting the ice clink against the glass, and meet Khalid's eyes. A subtle acknowledgment passes between us—a shared understanding—and Sierra's little jab feels more insignificant.

"Umm...Denise!" Sierra calls, her voice a little sharper than necessary, as if dragging someone else into the conversation might save her from the corner she's just backed herself into. I watch Denise turn toward her, eyebrows raised in curiosity, and Sierra immediately starts leaning in, talking over her shoulder as though the distraction can erase the tension she's created. I shake my head slightly, refusing to give her the comfort of looking away.

"Ou pa wont..." I murmur in Creole. Khalid leans in slightly, tilting his head, a small frown tugging at his features.

"Did I miss something?" I shake my head lightly, forcing a casual smile, though my tone is sharp.

"You didn't—but I think I missed the part where you're going to New York at the end of your contract." His eyes widen slightly, regret filling them for asking if he missed something.

"Wait...wait I was going to tell—wait, how did you—" he stammers, clearly caught off guard.

"Sierra," I say, cutting him off smoothly. Suddenly, a flicker of guilt washed over me. *Shit. Was I being too passive-aggressive by bringing it up like that?* "It's fine, Khalid," I added quickly, trying to ease the moment.

"No, no—please, Mia, let me explain," he says, stepping a little closer, urgency in his low tone. I shake my head gently, taking a small sip from my drink I've been babysitting like it's my companion.

"No, you don't have to. Honestly...I shouldn't have expectations, like I've always known you're on contract. Let's go back to your friends." I walk around him, heading back to the circle just a few steps away. He follows and we step a little further into the crowd, the hum of coworkers chatting and laughter swirling around us. I keep my phone in hand, letting it act as a buffer between us, giving me space to think as I nervously scroll on social media. I look up and watch him interact with his coworkers, almost trying to hide some kind of worry through half-laughs. Part of me felt bad that he obviously was distracted by what just happened. But another, sharper part of me stayed alert. The part that wanted answers. I glance down at my phone and, without another word to Khalid, I order an Uber.

"Baby, are you okay?" he asks quietly, catching my eye as he leans closer. His voice was low, but there was that undercurrent of worry I observe. I give a little shrug.

"I'm fine," I say, keeping my tone calm but firm. "But I think I'm going to head home for the night."

"Okay, we can—"

"No," I interrupt, careful with my tone. I push my drink in his hand that's not even halfway finished and look up at him. "You should stay. I think I want to head home alone." He frowns, stepping closer.

"I really don't want to let you go alone—we came together and—" I stop him mid-sentence.

"Trust me, it's fine," I manage to force a smile. I tip onto my toes, giving him a light quick kiss. "I'm a big girl. I tie my own sandals and everything." He blinks, caught off guard, a small smirk tugging at his lips despite himself.

"Baby, please, let me—" My phone chimes.

"Too late," I cut him off, glancing at the screen. "My Uber's here." He exhales sharply.

"Can we please talk? I know you're upset. Please give me a chance to explain, baby." I shift my bag over my shoulder.

"Sure," I say quietly. "Just...not tonight."

Khalid walks me to the Uber. I slide into the backseat of the car; the door clicks behind me. The driver greets me with a polite nod, and I return the gesture, distracted. Khalid bends to the window. He leans in, pressing a gentle unhurried kiss to my lips.

"Promise we'll talk?" he asks quietly, his forehead resting briefly against mine.

"Yes," I whisper. He nods, lingering for a moment then pulls back slightly.

"Please...let me know when you get home." I give a faint nod.

"I will."

As the car pulls away, I press my forehead lightly to the cool glass. I dab my cheeks lightly with the back of my head as though my makeup still needs to be preserved. I'm falling in love with him. So much for him initiating. What even is there to explain? I'm not a long-distance girl and he's leaving. If anything, it's time to distance myself.

# CHAPTER SEVENTEEN
## *Khalid*

I walk back to my coworkers, hands pressed to the back of my head, lingering like the weight of the evening is pressing me down. My mind spins, rewinding the last few minutes, thinking about how everything just got fucked up. Why the fuck did Sierra mention my contract at all? I can't stop running the scenario over in my head—how it looked, how dishonest I must have seemed. Coming from a random coworker and not from me. That should've come from me. I had every intention of telling her. Every single one. And honestly, even thinking about it feels conflicting—though I had planned to tell her about the New York contract my recruiter has been working on, deep down, I wanted to tell her I don't want to go. If she wanted me to, I would stay here. I would move my entire life out here for her. I'm falling in love with her, and I don't know if she feels the same.

James notices me staring off.

"Everything okay, bro?"

"Yeah...umm...I think I'm gonna head out though."

"Okay...did the pretty lady head out? I haven't seen her."

"Yeah. Mia took an Uber home." James pauses and stares at my for just a second as though he's searching for answers in my face.

"Aye, wanna link up for a workout tomorrow? You off, right?" He's such a solid homie.

"That sounds cool, man," I say shortly. "Let's link up at nine?"

"Sounds good, bro. I'll meet you then!"

We bump fists. I grab my motorcycle helmet and Mia's off the table, to head out, the night hit me like a wake-up call. The motorcycle engine is loud, but the sound doesn't drown out the noise in my head— the look on her face, the quiet hurt I put there. I push the throttle anyway, trying to outrun the guilt sitting heavy in my chest. But no matter how fast I go, I can't shake the truth beating through me—I don't want New York. I want to stay here, with her.

By the time I reach my place, the night is quiet. I grab my phone, almost expecting a text from her.

*Me: Hey...did you make it home okay?*

A moment passes.

*Mia: I did.. Have a good night.*

I stare at the screen, letting a small relief settle over me. She's being dry, I toss my helmet aside, sink onto the couch, and stare at the ceiling until sleep drags me under.

*

The morning sun peeps through the curtains, casting a light on my face.

I peel my eyes open, curtains, shocking myself to see that I'm still in the same clothes from last night and fell asleep on the couch. Worry pits in my stomach as I remember every detail that happened last night with Mia. I search for my phone around the couch pillows.

*James: Hey bro, just checking on you. We still down to meet at nine?*

*Me: Let's make it 9:30*

I go back to Mia's thread, thumb hovering over the screen. I don't want her to think I don't care by not texting, but I also want to respect her space. After a few rounds of back and forth with myself, I finally send her a message.

*Me: Hey Mia, I hope you slept okay.*

Taking a shower before the gym seems pointless, but I can't stand the smell of the outside on me. Quick rinse, toss on gym clothes, sling my bag over my shoulder, and head out. The sun hits my back. For a second, I let the tension from last night fade and focus on the steady rhythm of my footsteps.

*

The gym's already humming when I walk in—weights clanging, music coming through the speakers. James is by the dumbbells, grinning when he spots me.

"Bro! Thought you were about to bail," he says, fist out.

"Nah," I grin weakly, tapping his knuckles. "Just running slow this morning."

We start our warm-up sets, the usual small talk slipping in—music, work, whatever. But I can tell he's holding a question behind his eyes. After a few reps, he sets his weights down.

"So what happened last night? Why'd you and Mia leave separately?" I pause, exhaling.

"She found out about New York." He frowns.

"'Found out?' isn't that at the end of the month? Was that supposed to be a secret from her?"

"No, no." I drop my weights, the sound hitting louder than I mean it to. A couple of people glance over. I rub the back of my neck and let out a breath. "I meant to tell her. I just...I've been trying to figure out how to say it, let alone that New York is an option—but more than anything, I want to stay here. With her. Just been waiting for the right time." James blinks, eyes wide.

"Wait...are you serious, bro?"

"Yeah." I nod, leaning forward on my knees. "I've thought a lot about it and I've decided. I've never met anybody like her. I know a few months isn't a lot of time, but it's a chance I'm willing to take." James shakes his head, smiling.

"Man, that's beautiful. I'm happy for you, big dawg. But hold up—if you didn't tell her about New York, how did she find out?" I drag a hand down my face, frustration tightening my chest.

"Somehow Sierra knew. She must've overheard me talking to you about it at work that day, and she told Mia last night." James's eyes widen.

"You lying. That chick is way too deep in your business."

"She is," I say, exhaling hard. "But it's on me. I shouldn't have waited this long, I should've told Mia sooner. It's just been tricky—with time kind of against us, I didn't want to put her in a position where she felt like she had to say yes just after a few months of dating, I'd prefer for her to choose me freely, not out of pressure or timing. And I also don't expect her to ask me to. We never really talked about the future. I don't think either of us expected this and may have entered this thinking it was going to be short term and casual, but it ended up being so much more, at least for me. I need to know if she feels the same. I guess part of me was nervous to ask, because again, time." James studies me for a second, then nods slowly.

"Yeah, but sounds like you already know what you want that future to look like." I look down, setting the dumbbell between my palms.

"Yeah...I do." He grins, nudging my shoulder.

"I can't lie, bro, I'm happy to hear that you might be staying out here in Cali. You cool to work with, to hang out with. I got mad respect for you, man. For real." A small smile tugs at my lips.

"Appreciate you, man. Likewise." He nods.

"Don't trip about last night. You just gotta talk to her, that's all. Be real about it."

"Yeah," I say quietly, gripping the dumbbell a little tighter. "That's the plan."

I push through the last few reps until my arms shake. We finish up, wipe down the benches, and grab towels from the rack.

The walk out to the parking lot feels longer than it should. I check out thread to see if she texted me earlier. No new messages. I toss my gym bag in the back seat, lean against the bike for a second.

"Alright, I'll holla at you, bro!" I call out to James.

"Later, bro! Aye, you work tomorrow?"

"I do—night shift tonight and the next two."

"Cool, I'll see you then!" I nod, watching him head off before my eyes drift back to my screen. Mia's name stares back at me, the silence between us pressing heavier by the minute. I hover my thumb over the message bar.

*Me: Would you like to meet up today?*

Bubbles.

Then, no bubbles.

Finally—

*Mia: I would, but I have a lot of work to catch up on. Also, I think I have a stomach bug or something. I haven't been feeling well.*

*Me: No problem, I understand.*

I just want a chance to make things right. I'm so sorry about how things transpired. You weren't supposed to find out that way.

A minute passes.

*Mia: Honestly, I don't really know what to say right now. I'm not sure there's much to talk about. But...we can meet up sometime this week. I just need some time to clear my head. I feel like I've been reckless.*

I stare at her message a moment longer. I can tell she's hurting, and I hate that I'm the reason. Still, I don't want to push. Just let her know I care.

*Me: All right. I'm sending dinner to your door so you don't have to cook. Take your time. Take your space. I'm here if you need anything.*
*I just want a chance to make things right. I'm so sorry about how things transpired. You weren't supposed to find out that way.*

I switch over to the DoorDash app, scrolling until I find her favorite Pho soup spot. She loves that place when she's not feeling well. I type in her address, add extra lime and sriracha the way she likes it—and hit 'order.' It's not much, but it's something. A quiet way of saying I care and I want her to know I'm here.
Her reply pops up almost immediately.

*Mia: Thank you, I appreciate it.*

A small, quiet relief settles in my chest. No words needed beyond that for now. I toss my phone into the pocket of my jacket, swing my leg over the motorcycle, and grip the handles and head back to my spot.

When I pull into the Airbnb drive-way, I swing my leg off the bike and set it on the kickstand, reaching for my phone. A new text lights up the screen—my manager, Rob:

*Hey Khalid, We know your contract is ending soon. We also overheard from James that there's a chance you might contemplate staying. We just want you to know you have our full support, and if you're seriously considering it, we would love to schedule a meeting with you as we'd love to have you here on our team.*

I grin, shaking my head slightly. James...sneaky, in a good way. He's putting in a word for me without me even knowing. Looking out for me. That's the kind of homie he is. I let out a sigh of relief. Support. Choice. Options. Signs and confirmation. I tuck the phone in my pocket, and step inside, letting the quiet of my temporary residence welcome me.

# CHAPTER EIGHTEEN
## *Mia*

Ioversleep and wake to the taste of nausea crawling up my throat. The pho Khalid sent me helped a little, but by the time I get to the shop, the nausea's settled in like it paid rent. The morning rush comes and goes. Around lunchtime, a woman pushes her latte back across the counter with a tight smile.

"Sorry, but this seems...off? A bit burnt maybe?"

"Oh no, I apologize! Let me remake that for you, give me a few moments."

I move through the motions—steam, pour, swirl—nothing I haven't done a million times already. But halfway through, the hiss of the milk frother and the sharp smell of espresso makes my mouth water in that awful way that means run. I grip the edge of the counter, trying not to let it show. By the time I set her fresh cup down, I'm fighting to catch my breath.

"Thanks, sweetheart!" she chirps, oblivious. I force a smile.

"Of course. Have a good one."

The bell over the door jingles as she leaves. I lean back against the shelves behind me, pressing my palms to my temples.

My phone buzzes in my apron pocket. Khalid.

Khalid: How are you feeling?

I swallow down the taste in my throat and type back with shaky thumbs.

*Me: Hey. I'm fine, still feeling sick. And lethargic.*

*Khalid: Need me to come rescue you before I go to work?*

I almost laugh. He would try that—show up to shorten this space I'm carving out while I clear my head.

*Me: No, I'm okay. José is here. I'll rest when I get home. Thank you for the offer.*

I pocket my phone and catch José eyeing me from the back counter. "You good, Mia?" I nod too quickly.

"Yeah. Just a little off today. I'm fine." He raises a brow but doesn't push it. By three, I can't fake it anymore; José crosses his arms and plants himself in front of the register.

"Girl, Go home. Seriously. I got this. You look like you're about to pass out." I open my mouth to argue, but another wave of dizziness decides for me. I text Khalid with a status update.

*Me: Stomach bug 1, me 0. I'm heading home.*

*Khalid: I'm sorry, baby. Is there any medicine you're comfortable taking? I can send it to you.*

Even though I'm upset with him—and he knows that—he's so sweet. Always so sweet. I lean against the counter for a moment, staring at the floor. I know he wants to fix this. I know he wants to talk, to smooth over what went wrong. But I'm not ready—not yet. I don't know how I got here—or better yet, how I allowed myself to fall for someone that's leaving. I am not down for long distance. And I can't tell him that I'm falling for him exactly. Am I just supposed to hide how I feel and take it on the chin as we have this serious conversation about him leaving? And yet...I know putting it off won't make the conversation disappear. Sooner or later, we'll have to face it.

A few minutes later, my phone vibrates again.

*Khalid: Medicine is on the way to your place. Take your time. I'm here if you need anything.*

I let out a small, quiet breath. Even now, he's thinking about me, looking out for me. I don't answer right away—just sit with the feeling of being cared for, even if the hurt is still there.

I look at José and muster a tired smile.

"Thank you for covering for me, love. I owe you." He waves me off.

"You're good, girl. Get some rest."

I grab my bag and step out into the air that does absolutely nothing to settle my stomach. By the time I arrive to my townhome, the DoorDash driver is pulling away, my medicine waiting on the porch like a tiny blessing. I open the bag and find not just medicine but ginger tea. I crawl onto the couch, with a hot cup of ginger tea, and let Insecure reruns fill the quiet.

*Khalid: Baby how are you feeling? Is your nausea any better?*

*Me: So off. I'm just gonna head to bed early.*

*Khalid: No problem. Sleep well—text me if you need anything.*

I fall asleep to the TV, tea cold on the coffee table.

The next morning, I wake up before my alarm even thinks about nagging me. I drag myself to the bathroom for my morning routine. The coffee maker does its job and I pour a cup, and the first sip sends me running to the sink. I vomit so hard my knees buckle.

What the hell is wrong with me?

I brace my palms on the counter, breathing through it, ignoring the sour taste clinging to my tongue. I then go to wash my mouth out and brush my teeth again. For whatever reason, evening sticking the toothbrush in my mouth makes me want to hurl again.

Great, now I'll need a new tooth brush.

Before I can think too far, my phone buzzes on the edge of the sink.

*Reminder: Honey shipment arriving at 7:00 a.m. on the 30th.*

In that moment, my eyes grow wide as I realize it: I'm late.

And not by just a day or two, but by almost two weeks.

My heartbeat is loud in my ears and I feel like I'm going to vomit again but this time because of the anxiety I'm feeling. I grab my phone within seconds to order a pregnancy test via DoorDash. *"ETA 23 minutes..."* I press a hand to my belly, as if an answer might wait there. It felt like every minute I waited for the DoorDash shopper to deliver the pregnancy test to my door lasted a lifetime. I can't sit still. I move around the kitchen on instinct, filling the kettle, dropping slices of ginger into my favorite mug, adding a swirl of honey like it might somehow steady me. The steam rises in the air, but it does nothing for my nerves. I sip, pace, check my phone.

*18 minutes.* Pace again.

I feel like I'm waiting to watch water boil.

When the delivery ping finally lights up my screen, my breath snags. I wait a beat, maybe two, before tiptoeing to the door. I look through the peephole first—just making sure they're gone.

Something about a stranger knowing I ordered that feels strangely intimate, like they've seen a part of me I haven't even confirmed yet. But who am I kidding, so does checking out at the grocery store. Once the porch is clear I open the door, grab the small bag and head to my bathroom to do my business. The loading bar on the pregnancy test continues to flash on the screen. I feel frustrated just looking at it, it's taunting me. Maybe I'm not pregnant. Maybe it's a coincidence.

Nearly twelve days, *this happens ...doesn't it?*

Nervously, I take a large gulp of my water. I've been a little stressed and probably didn't realize it with so much business at the shop since Destiny has been out of town. I just need to take better care of myself. I've been saying that. More sleep. Get my body back in sync, and watch, in the next day or two my period will be—I gasp for air and immediately become lightheaded. The glass slips from my hand and shatters against the tile floor. Water splashes across my feet, and tiny shards scatter like spread confetti. I don't move. I can't. My hands fly to my mouth.

*Pregnant.*

The word stares back at me from the tiny screen like it's mocking me.

I blink. Hard. Once. Twice. But it doesn't go away.

I'm pregnant.

I sit down on the edge of the tub, still holding the test like it might transform into something else if I just stare long enough. This isn't happening. It can't be. He's leaving soon. This can't be happening. With barely a month left on his nursing contract, how is this happening?!

We've only been dating for just over five months. Five beautiful, unpredictable, whirlwind months. And I've fallen for him. Hard. Faster than I meant to and what I was ready for. I close my eyes, and I'm back on the waterfront with him. The kiss we shared. The love we made. I think of our fingers clasping together while in my bed and it sends chills down my back. I blink myself almost as if to transfer myself back to the present.

Now everything is different.

How do I tell him I'm pregnant when he's packing to go to leave? His ass didn't even bother to tell me about New York. We never even talked about the future—not like this. Favorite movies and childhood memories were the topics of our conversation. But a baby? I glance in the mirror, hoping my reflection will offer something—strength, answers, maybe just a little grace. All I see is nervousness and panic. I think of my floral shop. My little dream. It's just taking off, just breathing on its own. Can it support me and a baby?

Then, my sisters.

They've always been my biggest supporters. But this is so different—unexpected. A fling turned messy.

*What will they say?*

The worry settles into my chest like a weight I wasn't ready to carry. I touch my stomach gently, barely even thinking. I grab my phone and walk to my room, the test still clutched in my other hand like proof I didn't ask for. Lightheadedness hits me halfway across the floor—quick and dizzying—and I pause, steadying myself before sinking onto the edge of the bed.

I open my messages and stare at our thread. His name. His face in the little circle. The last thing he asked was, "Baby how are you feeling? Is your nausea any better?" That feels like a lifetime ago. My finger hovers over the call button, but I can't bring myself to go through with it. What will I say?

What will he say? I close out the screen and decide without thinking much further that I'm not dealing with this right now. I grab my sandals, notebook, and pen to head to the beach to clear my thoughts.

# CHAPTER NINETEEN
## *Mia*

I make my way down the stairs and find a spot where I'm alone, the same spot where I brought Khalid. Honestly, I brought myself to the beach just to cry. If Khalid doesn't want to be a part of this, can I handle it on my own? I'm thirty-two. I own my business. Is this what's next for me—this new chapter? Is this the path I'm supposed to be on? I feel so irresponsible asking myself these questions.

My phone buzzes. It's Sage. "Hiiiiiii, babyyyyyyy!" she sings through the phone as soon as I press accept.

"Hi, my love," I respond, my voice cracking. Her tone shifts instantly, sharp and concerned.

"Mia, what's wrong?"

"Sage..." I start, but before I can get another word in, the crying starts. I burst into tears.

"Mia! whatever's going on, whatever is happening—it's going to be okay," she says, steady and sure. More tears fall as I try to hold it together.

"It's okay," she reassures me softly. "Do you want to talk about it? There's absolutely no pressure." I take a few moments, staring blankly at the waves rolling in. Slowly, I pull the pregnancy test out of my purse and hold it up in front of the camera.

"Oh my goodness, Mia," Sage breathes out, her voice filled with gentle shock. "Okay, okay, listen," she continues. "I know you're feeling so many emotions right now. And I want you to know—every single feeling you have is valid." More tears stream down my face. "Sister, I want to remind you of your strength, how capable you are." she says quietly. Her words settle over me like a cozy blanket.

"Thank you, Sage. I really appreciate your comfort and your words," I say.

"Of course," she says. I take a breath, then look down at the test still in my hand.

"He doesn't know," I say quietly. "And his contract ends in less than three weeks. I just, I fear, I'm too far deep in the unknown than I should be. Like I've been reckless." Sage pauses for a moment on the other end. I can feel her energy shift—grounded, present.

"Mia...this baby chose your soul for a reason," she says, tender but sure. "You're not alone in this. You're protected. Your spirit guides are looking after you, the ancestors...hell, even your plants are probably leaning in right now. You are held, sis. I need you to know you are right where you should be in life." More tears slip down my cheek.

"You really believe that, Sage?

"Yes, of course I do. You know me—I do not front. I would not just be saying this if I didn't fully believe it. Mia, just listen to your body, your breath, your spirit. Ask for guidance and pace yourself. And claim ease in every moment of this." I wipe my face and stare out at the waves crashing in front of me.

"I was thinking to myself...what my life path is. What chapter I'm stepping into. I'm thirty-two. My shop's just standing on its own. And now, this..." I pause and take a deep breath. "I can't say I'm ready. But, I'm in this." The tears finally stop.

"That's my girl!" Sage says, cheering me on. She sets the phone down and I see her clapping for me. Her support makes my eyes get watery again.

"That's the strength that changes bloodlines."

"Thank you, Sage. I love you deeply."

"I love youuuuu, no need to thank me. This is all for you. That baby is already blessed. And you?" Her voice softens. "You're going to be an amazing mother, Mia. I know it." I smile.

"I appreciate you so much. I'm not gonna lie though, the thought of telling Khalid makes me want to pass out."

"Listen," she says gently, "we don't know how he'll respond. So instead of spiraling into the unknown, let's choose ease. I know that's easier said than done—but just breathe, boo. You don't have to carry it all at once." Then, in true Sage fashion, she adds, "And worst case? We'll do a gender reveal and a man reveal. Invite everybody, let the spirits sort 'em out." I laugh, finally.

"Thank you," I say again, lighter this time.

"Always, mama. Always." she says.

"Before we hang up...How are you feeling? You look so radiant, sis," I say, wiping the last of my tears.

She shifts the camera, and I see her belly: small, round, growing. My chest tightens in awe, and all the worry I've been carrying suddenly lifts. I can't help but rest my hand on my own stomach, feeling a quiet connection between the two little lives growing before us. I'm captivated by the miracle unfolding before me.

I grasp the phone tighter and hold it closer to see.

"Sage..." I whisper, my voice trembling with wonder. "Look at you. I'm just in awe...of you, and of this little life you're carrying." She laughs, resting a hand over her bump.

"I feel so grateful, Mia. Every day I get to feel her, to watch her grow... It's humbling. And now that the nausea has chilled out and I have more energy in this second trimester. I was great before, but now I'm even better." I close my eyes for a moment, letting the relief settle through me.

"I'm so excited for you, sis. Seeing you like this...it makes everything feel more real, more possible. I'm so happy for you. I love you, and I already love this little one too!" Her gaze turns tender.

"We'll do this together, Mia. Every step, every trimester...you're not alone." I squeeze my own stomach, feeling both awe and anticipation.

"I already can't wait to meet her. I love you both so much." Sage grins.

"The feelings are so mutual, sis. I won't keep you on the phone any longer now—I know you have some things to process, so I'll give you the space to do that. Hubby also booked me a prenatal massage appointment so I'll need to get ready to head out soon, but if you need anything at all, I'm only one call away." I laugh, the tension melting a little.

"Okay, Chingy!" I say laughing. "And I love how your man is taking care of you, sissy, especially during pregnancy—it warms my whole heart. Okay, okay, there I go starting over, Love you always, boo," I reply. We both crack up, the sound comfort and familiarity over the line. "Love you, sis" I add in a small voice.

"Thank you, sissy, and love you, too!" she says. We hang up then, but I'm still smiling long after the call ends.

*He deserves to know, doesn't he? But what if his response breaks me?*

I press my hand gently against my lower stomach. This is real. No matter what happens. No matter what he says. This life inside me...is mine now. And maybe that's where I start. Not with panic. Not with pressure. But with truth. He deserves that, and so do I. I gather my things and stand up slowly, taking one last look at the waves before I turn to go. I make my way up the stairs and stop in the middle of the steps. I pull out my phone and stare at the screen for a moment, my thumb hovering. Then I open our thread.


*Me: Hey...are you home right now? I was wondering if I could come over for a little.*


I hit send before I can overthink it. If he says no, I'll handle it. If he says yes...well, I'll take that next breath when it comes.

***Khalid:** Hey, yeah, I am. What's up?*

The lump in my throat forms fast as my fingers type on the keyboard.

***Me:** Can I come over?*

***Khalid:** Of course, I work the night shift tonight but I don't start till 7:30. Is everything okay?*

I stare at the screen. It's currently 6:15 p.m.

Instead of answering, I get into my car and the music cuts on automatically—some upbeat song that feels like it belongs in someone else's world, and it immediately annoys me. I reach for the dial and turn it off. I can't handle noise right now. I pull out of the parking lot and onto the road, looking at the sky's hues of a fading sunset. It's absolutely stunning—lavender skies melting into orange and gold—but it feels distant, like beauty I can't quite reach. The nausea that's lingered all day rises again, this time stronger. It curls in my stomach. I grip the steering wheel tighter, breathe slow through my nose. I don't want to cry again. I don't want to fall apart before I get there.

I'm not afraid of him. I'm afraid of what this might change. Of what it means to say the words out loud. I'm afraid that no matter how gentle or kind or present he's been...this could shake everything.

And even though I wouldn't be alone—my sisters have always been in my corner—it still isn't the way I saw this going. I envisioned this with my person. A shared joy. A knowing that we'd figure it out together. If he wants no part of this...it would break my heart.

As I get closer to his place, the ache in my chest deepens. Tears slide silently down my cheeks. I swipe them away, but they keep falling. I reach a familiar intersection and slow down.    A    four-way    stop. Quiet. Empty. I glance left, then right.

Clear. I ease forward.

And then it all happens so fast—

Blinding headlights steal my vision. I notice a blur from the left. A car runs the stop sign. Too fast for me to think, too fast for me to move out of the way. The car rams the passenger side of my car. Metal and tires screech. The impact causes the glass to explode at the same time as the airbags deploy.

My body jolts and my head slams into my door. A high-pitched ringing in my ears blasts as I drift in and out of consciousness. Voices call out, muffled but insistent.

"Miss, are you okay??? Someone call 911!"

I try desperately to keep my eyes open, but I lose the battle.

# CHAPTER TWENTY
## *Khalid*

I glance at my phone again. No new messages.

*I don't get it. I replied immediately, telling her to come, and asked if everything was okay and got no response. It's been over thirty minutes. Maybe there's traffic...*

I try to brush off the unease creeping into my chest. I pace around my room, glancing out the window every few minutes, hoping to see her car. It's 6:55 p.m. and I have to leave for work soon. I pick up my phone, contemplating whether to call her. But I don't want to press her; She's been feeling off all day. And we still haven't chatted since the whole Sierra–New York ordeal.

*Fuck it.*

I call her anyway: the line rings and rings.

*"Hi, it's Mia. You've missed me, but leave a message and I'll call you back or send a text—it's much faster!"*

I end the call before the voicemail begins and finish packing the rest of my things, then pull out my phone to text her:

*Me: Baby, I have to leave for work now. Call me when you can. I'll try to answer.*

There's an urge in me to end that sentence with I love you, but I resist. Still, my mind won't stop spinning.

*What did she want to meet up about all of a sudden? Maybe she wanted to discuss the end of my contract?*

We've always been in the moment leading up to now. I just know there's no one else I'd rather be with. I want her to feel comfortable not pressured. Maybe I can get my own apartment? I shake my head, almost as if to shake off the ambiguity that's beginning to upset my stomach. I glance at my phone again. It's now 7:15 p.m. Still no messages. I grab my book bag and head out the door to head to work.

*

I arrive at the hospital and get myself clocked in and ready for first rounds. Before heading to my first patient's room, I call Mia one more time.

Ring...

"Hi, it's Mia—" Click.

"Damn, where is this girl?" I mumble under my breath.

I make my way down the hall when I spot Sierra. She freezes when she sees me.

"Hey," she says, lowering her voice.

"What's up, Sierra?" I say with zero expression in my face.

"I just—wanted to say sorry. If I caused anything between you and her.

I nod. "It's fine." And I mean it.

She gives a tight smile, already stepping back.

"When you got here, I liked you an embarrassing amount," she admits, "and I acted out of character. That's not who I am, I may talk shit for fun or be petty jokingly but I got carried away and had been drinking...that's my bad."

I don't say anything. Immaturity like this repulses me and I don't have the capacity to discuss it any further just to make her feel better about herself. The silence stretches. She glances around the hallway, avoiding my eyes, shifting her weight like she suddenly regrets saying it out loud.

"Take care, Khalid."

"You as well Seirra."

She walks away and I turn the opposite direction to turn the corner and make my way down the hall until I hear it—some kind of commotion: fast footsteps, urgent voices. A stretcher barrels down the hallway, surrounded by nurses. I glance over only casually at first, but then my breath catches at the sight of something unexpectedly familiar: a dark head of hair, with an unmistakable mass of curls.

No. No. *No.*

# CHAPTER TWENTY-ONE
## *Mia*

My eyes fly open. I try to sit up, but a firm hand rests on my shoulder, easing me back.

"Easy," a voice says gently. "You're okay, baby. You're in the hospital. You were in a car accident. But we got you, it's okay; you're going to be fine."

A nurse, mid-forties, checks the monitors beside me and my IV. I try to sit up again. My body protests instantly.

"Pregnant..." I whisper. "Is the baby..."

"You're still early—right? We're going to monitor everything closely. The doctor will be in soon to explain more, but for now, you're stable. That's a significant sign." I take a deep breath. The nurse glances toward the door, then back at me with a flicker of recognition.

"Your boyfriend's here. He works in the ER—Khalid? He was just down the hall when the paramedics brought you in." My stomach drops.

*Khalid.* Here. Of course. This is *his* hospital.

"I'll give you some privacy," she says gently, showing herself out of the room before I can ask her to wait.

Seconds later, the door opens. And there he is. He's in his scrubs. ID badge clipped to his chest, eyes wide of something between fear and disbelief. His gaze roams over me—my face, the IV in my arm, my throbbing head, the heart monitor—and then lands back on my eyes. Only his eyes are glistening.

"I didn't know what happened," he says, stepping closer, voice at a tremble. "All this time I was wondering why I didn't hear from you after you asked to come over...I was going to go to your place in the morning if I didn't hear from you by then." He wipes a tear from his cheek, quickly and ungracefully. "I thought I...I thought I lost you." I open my mouth, but nothing comes out. My throat is thick, and I feel the urge to burst into tears. "You're not my patient so I couldn't check your chart," he adds. "Can you tell me what happened?" he asks, eyes searching mine. I nod, barely.

"Someone ran a stop sign. I didn't see them until it was too late; their car hit my passenger side." His jaw clenches, his hands balling into fists at his sides then lets out a sigh.

"Damn Mia. I'm so thankful you're here and okay. I was in the ER when they brought you in. I saw you being brought in—" he stops, pressing his lips together. "I felt like I couldn't breathe." His hand reaches for mine, hesitant at first, like he's afraid I'm fragile and it will hurt me. Our fingers lace together. There's so much I want to say, but the words sit heavy in my chest. So I don't. I need to tell him I'm pregnant. But not tonight. Not after everything that just happened.

Khalid's work phone rings. He sighs, checking the screen.

"I've got to check on my patients. I'm on a different floor," he says. "But I'll take you home as soon as they discharge you." He lingers for a second longer. "Just rest for now, and don't hesitate to call me. I'm not able to be your nurse... but I'm still looking out for you." A small smile rises.

"Thank you," I whisper. He leans down and presses a kiss to my forehead. And makes his way out of the room. I rest my head back and within moments, my eyes drift and I fall asleep.

"Alright," the doctor says, flipping through the chart on her tablet. "It's been over twelve hours since you were last admitted, and your scans came back clear—no internal bleeding, just a concussion and a couple of bruises. By the looks of the car, you're lucky." I nod slowly, my head still spinning from everything that's happened.

"It's also my understanding that you declined any pain medication because of your pregnancy, correct?"

*Pregnant.* The word echoes through me like a distant bell—still hard to believe.

"Yes," I whisper. She gives a small, understanding nod.

"We'll note it in your chart. Just follow up with your OB as soon as possible. Baby has a strong heartbeat, but still, it's important we monitor." She pauses for a beat. "Do you have someone to take you home?"

"Yeah. I do. He should be here any minute."

"Okay. Keep resting, stay hydrated, and try to take it easy for the next few days—physically and emotionally." Her tone eases. "And if anything feels off, come back in, alright?"

"Okay. Thank you."

She gives me a small smile, then gently pulls the curtain back and slips out. I exhale, sinking deeper into the pillows. My hands drift to my stomach, it's hard to believe there's something growing there. Something real. Something mine. I close my eyes. And let it all settle. I still need to tell Khalid. As if on cue, the curtain rustles again, and Khalid steps inside—quiet and careful. He's out of his scrubs and back in normal clothes. He looks like something's on his mind.

"Ready to go home?" he asks gently. "I rented a car for the week," he adds. "Didn't want you riding on the bike while you're achy."

"Thank you," I say, then pause. "That reminds me—I'll need to sort things out with my insurance."

"There's no rush," he says. "I just wanted to make sure you're taken care of." He walks over and helps me sit up slowly, his hand steady at my back. "You okay?" he asks.

"I think so, just kinda sore," I murmur, eyes flicking to my stomach for a second. "Still trying to catch up to everything." He reaches into a bag and pulls out a hoodie.

"I brought you something cozy." I smile.

"Thank you, I really appreciate it."

# CHAPTER TWENTY-TWO
## *Khalid*

We pull up at her house from the hospital and walk inside. The car ride was quiet; she closed her eyes the entire time. The air between us feels heavy—like both our minds are racing, but neither of us wants to start first. She drops her purse and hospital paperwork on the entryway table, keys clinking against the wood. Mia heads to the shower. I busy myself in the kitchen, trying to make myself useful. I grab her favorite mug and fix her some ginger tea the way she likes it—with honey instead of sugar. Then, I wrap an ice pack in a towel and set it on the coffee table. By the time I've pulled up *Insecure* on the TV, she's walking out of the bathroom in her red mumu, satin bonnet tied snugly over her hair, skin noticeably glowing under the soft living room light.

"Trying to spoil me?" she teases weakly, her voice small but playful.

"I just wanna take care of you," I say, handing her the mug. "Make sure you're good." She sinks onto the couch with a fluffy throw blanket, curling her legs beneath her, tea cradled in her hands. I sit beside her—not too close yet, just enough to feel her warmth near mine. For a few minutes, we let the show fill the silence—both of us pretending to watch but neither of us really there.

Eventually, I can't sit on it any longer. My chest feels too tight.

"Mia…" She hums in acknowledgment, eyes still on the screen. "I need to talk to you," I start. "And I don't want to press you—I know you asked for space after what happened with Sierra, and we're just getting home from the hospital—" She turns slowly, one hand still on her mug.

"It's fine," she says quietly. "We can talk." Her eyes flick up to mine, nervous but open.

"Baby, it's okay—I didn't mean that we have to do this right now, I was only saying at some point—"

"No, let's talk." She sets the mug down and sighs. "I didn't mean to push you away. I just…I was confused." She pulls the blanket over her lap, bracing herself.

"Ask me anything you need to," I say. "I can explain everything." She exhales.

"Your contract ending…I knew it was coming. And I don't care about Sierra, obviously. I was just…irritated. Finding out from your coworker that you're going across the country—Khalid, that hurt." Her voice cracks a little, and I hate myself for it.

"I know this was supposed to be temporary. I knew not to have expectations, but damn—you could've told me where you were going. Serious or not…" She stops, shaking her head. "How I felt about you caught me by surprise and…actually, never mind."

"Baby, wait." I lean forward, elbows on my knees. "I need to say this now—because if I leave without telling you what's been on my heart, I'll never forgive myself." She looks up at me, eyes already glossy.

"Yes, New York was in the works," I say, steadying my voice. "But what I've really been trying to find is the perfect moment to tell you how deeply I'm in love with you." Mia's lips part slightly. She doesn't speak, but she doesn't look away either. "There's something about you that brings me a kind of happiness I can't explain. I've had people come and go in my life, but you? You're the kind that brings me peace. The way our souls and spirits align…it's like God gave me the love I didn't even know how to ask for." Mia swallows. One of her hands touches her stomach without thinking. I don't know if she even notices. "I feel at peace with you. Your smile—lawd, your smile—was the first thing that pulled me in. Then your eyes. And your mind? That's what keeps me here, keeps me coming back for more. There's no doubt in me that God has more in store for us. And I want you to know: If you want me, I'm here to stay." I move closer to her. "Mia...you are everything to me. And I just hope I can be the same for you."

She covers her mouth as tears fall.

"Khalid...that's the most beautiful thing anyone has ever said to me." She pauses, her voice catching. "But...what about the contract? What about Florida and your family, Khalid I need you to know, if we do this, I'm not built for long distance or anything temporary. I—"

"Temporary? No Mia, forget the contract. New York is there, yes, but only if you didn't want to continue what we have. And I'm sorry for waiting so long to tell you. The truth is, I just didn't want you to feel pressured; I wasn't entirely sure how you felt. That's why it took me so long. Mia, I want to be with you. They're hiring here for permanent positions, and my manager has already reached out to me about it. I wouldn't ask you to leave your business behind. If you want me to stay—if you want to share a life together—let me be yours. We can do this. For real." Her eyes well up again. She hesitates, like she's holding something delicate that might shatter.

"Okay, wait—Khalid...I've been carrying something I need to tell you." She gently reaches for my hand.

"Okay, baby. Is everything alright?" I ask. She nods uncertainly. Then, she exhales, trembling just slightly.

"I—I'm pregnant." I stare at her, the words landing with quiet weight. And then I pull her into me. Tight. "I'm so sorry," she whispers into my shoulder. "I don't even know what to say. I wasn't trying to trap you or anything—I swear I wasn't." Tears stream from her eyes. She pulls back, but I hold her closer.

"Baby..." My voice cracks as my eyes blur, tears gathering fast. "You've made me the happiest man in the world. I mean that. Truly I do." Her breath catches, as if she's been holding it all day. I cup her face in both hands and look her straight in the eyes. "You think I'd run from something we created together? I would be a fool if I fumbled it. I love you, I want all of it—with you." She lets out a shaky sob, her forehead leaning into mine.

"Khalid, I love you, too...but I'm scared," she admits.

"I know," I whisper. "Me too. But I'm not going anywhere. Not now. Not ever." We sit there in the middle of her living room like the entire world just got rewritten around us. And then—because I can't help it—I brush a tear from her cheek and grin a little.

"You know our kid is about to have the strongest curls and the most stubborn attitude. That baby's doomed." She lets out a watery laugh and pats my chest.

"I can't stand you."

"But you love me though," I say smiling. She nods, still sobbing.

"I do—I'm in love with you, Khalid."

# CHAPTER TWENTY-THREE
## *Mia*

(One month later)

"Are you excited?" Destiny asks eagerly, practically bouncing in her seat. "I'm so excited—

we've got a niece or nephew on the way!"

"Honestly, it still doesn't feel totally real yet," I say, resting a hand on my belly. "I'm just so relieved the bleeding stopped. The hematoma had us so worried, especially because we didn't know how the car accident affected my body."

"I get it, the first trimester is so delicate; that's why it's often advised to wait till the second trimester to tell people. Not to mention what your body went through with the car accident and the bleeding that was happening. It was all very scary, it seemed hard to be in the moment, I'm sure." Prue says from the driver's seat. "Also, did the headaches post-concussion simmer down?"

"They have thankfully, for a few weeks I was getting them nearly every day, but I think now I get a headache maybe once a week if at all. I noticed I'm way more sensitive to light though."

"Continue to drink a ton of water and that tea I put together for you, remember at least three times a week," Prue says in a motherly way.

"Yes, ma'am," I say with a smile. "Also, Prue, when did you really feel pregnant?"

"Being pregnant didn't really hit me until I was further into my second trimester. That's when it sank in."

"You guys are so brave; pregnancy scares me! Anyway, I want to paint your nursery!" Destiny blurts out. I laugh.

"Oh my gosh, Destiny—that would be amazing. If you're really down..."

"Of course I am!" she says, like it's already decided.

"That reminds me—I need to give you all my maternity books," Prue adds. "I saved them."

"Thanks for keeping them, sis, I'll actually read them." We pull up in front of the store.

"Alright, hop out here so you don't have to walk far in the rain," Prue says. "Destiny and I will park and meet you inside."

"Sounds good," I say, unbuckling my seatbelt.

I slip out of the car and walk through the sliding doors, shaking off a few drops of rain. Inside, I head straight for the baby aisle. I stop when I see a pair of tiny brown moccasins—soft suede, barely the length of my palm. I run my thumb along one of them. I don't even know what size babies wear when they're born, but something about these feels special.

Then I hear it: A familiar voice that I haven't heard in so long.

"Wow! I never imagined running into you here!" I turn around to face her and immediately want to vomit. What are the odds I would run into my stepsister here and now?

"Hi, Angie," I say flatly. Her eyes widen as if she's just seen a ghost—or a camera.

"Oh my God...are you—?" Her gaze drops to my stomach. "Wow. I mean...you're glowing. I don't bother replying. I just place the shoes back on the shelf and reach for a different pair. She lingers.

"I didn't expect to see you here. I'm picking up some cute clothes as a gift for Eva's birthday. How far along are you? You're what—like a few months?" Her voice is sugary, but her eyes flicker with something else.

"Barely past my first trimester." I say dryly. I think about the car accident and the bleeding I experienced after. I truly thought I had miscarried, but thankfully the bleeding stopped and the baby is still growing healthy. I'm not telling her about that though; I never even told my dad about the accident. She steps closer.

"I'm just...surprised, that's all. You mentioned nothing. Does Dad even know?"

"Not yet," I say, voice steady and cool. "I plan to tell him in my way." Angie lets out a half-laugh.

"Of course. I mean, I just figured he should know, you know? I mean that baby would suffer without a grandparent!"

*Suffer*...Already speaking negativity on my baby. I feel rage spark in me and inhale slowly before I say something I can't take back.

"Angie," I say, measuredly, "I never said he would not find out—I said I'm going to tell him on my time, and in my way, I had some complications but now that it's fine, I'm telling him this week. I'm putting tiny booties in a box with a letter that I'm going to give to him. I really hope you don't say anything and just let me have this moment with my father. This isn't gossip." Her eyes flicker.

"Oh my goodness, how can you say that? You should know I'm trustworthy! I would say nothing to hurt you—I care about you, and this family. And the box idea is beautiful. I just think keeping secrets like this can get messy, especially with family. You know how emotional Dad can get..."

I glance at her. She always does this—takes what's not hers and coats it in concern. But her concern is never real. It's performance.

"I get what you're saying. It's not meant to be messy—I just wanted to get past my first trimester as I had some complications I'd rather not discuss—but now that we're past it, I'm comfortable to share the news." I reply. Then I give her the out: "Thank you for keeping this between us."

"Of course! Well, have a great day," she says brightly. "Remember, we're all part of your village, you're not alone!"

"Have a nice day, Angie." I turn and walk away, peace intact and no desire to stay in that conversation. But the unsettled feeling in my stomach grows. I really hope she doesn't tell my father. We may not be as close as we used to be, but I would be crushed if she took this moment from me. She always makes herself the messenger to Dad and my stepmom to be the favorite in her eyes. Her need for their validation is wild and the things she'll do to get it is even wilder. Like the time my nephew packed a T-shirt that didn't fit him and Prue didn't realize he packed it. She turned it into a whole announcement—pointed it out in front of everyone just so she could offer hand-me-downs and said "Joshua! These are very expensive!". It wasn't help—it was a performance. One of those moments where her voice gets all sweet and generous on the surface, but underneath, it's laced with subtle judgment. A quiet kind of mom-shaming of my sister Prue that she thinks no one notices. My nephew came home and vocalized his embarrassment because she said it in front of everyone.

Or the seafood boil incident. My nephew had crab before, just not the whole seafood boil shebang—she made a big production out of it. All wide-eyed and exaggerated: "Wait, he's never had seafood like this? Can you believe it? Did you guys ever make crab at your mom's house?"—again with the subtle shaming and belittling. It's strange and confusing, she would do so many sweet and thoughtful acts of kindness for others only to ruin it completely by talking too much. And by talking too much, she revealed it was never about kindness, it was never about being genuine. The cognitive dissonance is real. But the moment everything really shifted—the straw that broke it all—was when she tried to get me to confront Prue. Prue, my nephew's mom. Someone Angie hadn't spoken to in years wanted me to challenge Prue's no-sleepover rule. As if I had any business doing that. As if I was supposed to go against a mother's boundaries over a child that isn't even mine—just to prove some strange, performative loyalty.

And Prue wasn't being unreasonable. Her and my nephew's father's rule was clear from day one: hangouts between the kiddos, yes. Sleepovers, no. In Haitian culture this is the bottom line, no exceptions.

She kept calling it "getting the family together," like this was about unity. But later, the truth slipped out—it wasn't the sleepover, and it wasn't my nephew. She was spiraling because she thought Prue didn't like her, and in her mind that meant she couldn't hold the image she's always trying to project to everyone else to be liked. Angie performs, constantly. Always curating how she's seen. When that image doesn't land the way she wants, even something small becomes a crisis. When I tried to have a real conversation about it, explaining I couldn't believe I would ever be expected to challenge another mother's policies on their child—Angie doubled down. Looked me in the eye and said, "Well, we just want to know that you ride for us!"

*Us.*

Like this was a team sport. Like respect and boundaries didn't matter as long as she could feel chosen. That's when I knew—we weren't ever going to be a family. Because if you can't respect someone's parenting— if you can't stay in your lane—you're not trying to build a family. You're trying to build control.

"There you are!" Destiny says, walking up with Prue. "We tried calling you."

"Ohh my god," I say, still trying to shake off the interaction. "You will not believe who I just ran into." They both pause, already bracing.

"Who?" they ask in unison.

"Angie." Destiny gasps.

"No!" Prue's eyes narrow.

"Did you guys speak?"

"Well...she knows I'm pregnant."

"You told her?!" they both say at once.

"Of course not—she just put two and two together. I asked her not to tell Dad," I say, voice low. "I'm planning to tell him later this week. I just wanted to make it past the first trimester. Especially after all the bleeding in the beginning...I didn't want to speak too soon." Prue shakes her head.

"I don't trust her. She's a snake. Always smiling in your face, always keeping score."

"Neither do I, but weaponizing my pregnancy news wouldn't just be a crazy violation of privacy, that kind of performative bullshit would be more damaging than outright malice. I know she's a lot of things and needs to be the center of Dad and his wife's attention but that would be a whole different evil I hope she doesn't have in her. She also made some comment about being part of my 'village,'" I say, rolling my eyes. "And the way she said it...like I'd be alone." Prue crosses her arms.

"I hope she doesn't either. And to be clear, you don't owe anyone access; this is your child. I know how these people are—they don't like me because I set firm boundaries."

"Exactly," Destiny adds. "They operate with zero limits. It's strange. But you have an actual village—right here. Us. You don't need to manage her feelings on top of everything else."

"Thank you guys, and I know I have you. It's just so weird, they always try to make it seem like without them, I'm screwed. Even though they bring so much drama." Destiny laughs.

"'But what if I don't want to live the way you live?'" she says, quoting *The Devil Wears Prada*.

"'Oh, don't be ridiculous, Andrea, everybody wants this!'" I shoot back. We all start cracking up, then—our inside jokes never get old.

"We got you," Destiny says, giving me a light squeeze. "Let's pick out some cute little clothes for the baby. You're making new memories now. Don't let her mess that up." And with that, my sisters and I link arms and continue our day.

# CHAPTER TWENTY-FOUR
## *Mia*

The shop is closed on Mondays, which means it's just me, the faint scent of dried lavender, and the low hum of the refrigerator in the back. I sit at the bar counter with a small box in front of me, carefully placing the last of the tissue paper over a folded ultrasound photo and a pair of tiny beige booties. My hands hover for a moment before I add a short note on top:

*I know we've had our differences, but I want to believe there's room for something new between us. I'm excited for the memories we'll make and the ways we'll grow as we welcome your grandbaby into the world. I hope this marks the beginning of a softer chapter for us. Being a daddy's girl has never left my heart. I still think of you every time I hear "Iris" by the Goo Goo Dolls. I love you dearly and always will—and I hope you'll be part of this next chapter.*

I read it once more, then fold it and tuck it gently inside before tying the twine around the box. My stomach flutters with a strange mix of hope and nerves.

When my dad walks in a few minutes later, the little bell above the door chimes and glance at him. He looks around the shop, his hands buried deep in his jacket pockets.

"Hey, Dad," I say, managing a small smile. "Thanks for coming." He nods, his expression unreadable.

"Hey, baby...you said you wanted to talk."

"I did." I motion to the table near the window. "Come sit. I made some coffee if you'd like." He shakes his head.

"No, that's okay. I had some already." I grab the box and follow him to the table, setting it down between us as we take our seats.

"Okay umm, um, let's sit. I have something for you," I say, settling into the seat across from him and placing the box on the table between us. My dad has this odd half-smile on his face, like he's trying to hide something big. He looks at the box for a long moment.

"You gonna open it?" I ask, trying to stay calm. He lifts the lid slowly. Inside is a tiny pair of baby shoes and a folded ultrasound photo. He barely blinks.

"Oh! Um...wow, congratulations."

That's it. No breath caught. No wide eyes. Just...acceptance. As if he already knew. My stomach turns as I shift in my seat.

"You knew," I say quietly. "Angie told you." He sighs, not even bothering to deny it.

"She thought I deserved to know."

"I deserved to be the one to tell you," I snap. "That was *mine*. That was my moment, Dad."

"Mia, don't make this bigger than—"

"Bigger than what?" My voice cracks as heat rises in my chest. "She shared something that wasn't hers. That wasn't her story. For goodness' sake, this is *not* her baby— it's *mine*. And you—you're defending her?" He shifts uncomfortably.

"Mia, your attitude toward this family needs to be put in check... sometimes it makes it impossible to see anything else. She's my daughter too. I'm not saying it was her place—but maybe she thought she was helping. Maybe she thought you wouldn't tell me."

"Helping?" I say, my voice sharp and indignant. "You call that helping? Hijacking the most sacred part of my life to score points with you and your wife?" His jaw tightens.

"Mia...don't start. You need to learn some respect! You always jump to attack everyone instead of seeing their side! You don't understand what she's dealing with. Her husband has been back on the prowl again...messing with things he shouldn't. Being inappropriate with your eldest stepsister Kiana. She didn't mean harm."

"Remind me why we're protecting her feelings again?" I lean in, furious now. "You *always* do this. You'd rather pick apart the way I react than hold people accountable for what they do."

"Mia, come on—"

"*No.* No more excuses. She gave this speech about being trustworthy. And I believed her. And she ran out and turned my baby into gossip. It wasn't a celebration. It wasn't love. My baby was used as leverage." He looks down, still unable to speak. "I told her I wanted to wait. I was experiencing bleeding and was scared that—" I say, voice quieter now and I feel a knot forming in my throat thinking about how I thought I miscarried after the accident happened. "I told her about the box with the booties and the letter, She said that it was beautiful. Knowing damn well she was going to go behind my back." Silence hangs between us, thick. He stares at me now, speechless. "You always talk about boundaries, but you don't know what it means to respect them. If this had been me—if I'd done something even close to this—I'd be the black sheep declared by you and your wife until further notice." He rubs his hands together, sighing.

"Alright, Mia—I hear you, okay?" He pauses. "You're right."

I blink. *Wait—did I hear that correctly?*

"I've spent a long time choosing silence when I should've spoken up." He sighs again and rubs the back of his neck. "Letting things slide instead of protecting you. You're right—I defend her more than I should. I make excuses. I don't know why I do, I just do. It's not fair, it's not right, and I have no good reason for it." The lump in my throat burns. "I'm sorry, Mia. You're right. Angie was wrong. And coming here, pretending to be surprised, basically playing into that manipulation...I'm sorry." He looks at me then, eyes full of something heavy. "I don't expect things to go back to normal. I know they won't. But I hope I can be better moving forward. I owe you that." I stare at him. For once, he looks like he means what he says. But apologies don't rewind time. My father lets out a slow breath, eyes tracing the rim of the box. "So...Where do we go from here?"

I look at him—really look at him. For once, there wasn't anger in my chest. Just tiredness.

Acceptance. Clarity.

"Obviously, it's not my intention to keep you away," I say. "You're more than welcome to be in your grandbaby's life. I'm willing to start over with you...whatever that looks like. But this constant wave of drama? It's too much—for anyone. And the last thing I want is to bring our baby into that kind of negativity." He nods slowly, the smallest light of hope in his eyes. "But," I continue, my voice firmer now, "as for Angie—I don't ever want her around my child." His brow lifts.

"But...Angie—" I tilt my head.

"Oh, that wasn't a question," I say sternly. He sighs, frustration flickering behind his eyes.

"There you go again with this attitude! Mia, she's part of the family. She made a mistake, but she's still your stepsister, and she cares about you. Cutting her out completely is just wrong."

"Words can't express how much I don't care," I shoot back. "Some things don't get to be swept under the rug just because time passed, and sharing my pregnancy with you is something I'll never get back. She took that from me."

He opens his mouth, then closes it again, his jaw tightening. For a moment, I think he's about to argue again. But then something in his expression shifts—as if he's realized he's already lost too much trying to defend what didn't deserve defending.

"I may not like it," he says finally, voice lower, heavier. "But I have to accept it. You're the parent." He pauses, rubbing a hand over his face. "Mia, just know that I love you. I do. I've messed up. I'm not perfect, but I hope you'll let me in. Prue and I barely have a relationship as is, and I don't want that to happen with us too."

"I do, Dad. I don't expect you to be perfect," I reply. "And I love you, too."

Just then, Khalid walks in. I glance up at him as he comes through the door. My father turns around to see him for the first time.

"Good afternoon, sir," Khalid says, his voice steady and respectful. He rests his hand on my shoulder. My father stands to shake his hand.

"Pleasure to meet you, son. You must be Khalid."

Their hands meet in a firm handshake—but it's the look they exchange that says the most. Khalid holds his gaze just a second longer, his eyes calm but unflinching. My fathers facial expression falters, shadowed with something like shame. It's a silent exchange: *I know everything.* My father nods faintly, the way someone does when they've been seen and can't escape. "Thank you," he adds quietly. "For being part of my daughter's life. For standing beside her." Khalid gives a small nod.

"There's nowhere else I'd rather be." My dad looks at me, and for the first time, I think he really sees me. He clears his throat and straightens up slightly.

"Well...sounds like you two have a lot ahead of you. Have you already found a place or are you going to stay at the townhouse?"

"We're going to be moving into a bigger place," I say. He nods.

"You'll be a wonderful mom." This catches me off guard. I blink, unsure what to say, but Khalid gently squeezes my hand reassuringly beneath the table.

"And I'll do better," my dad adds, eyes on me now. "I don't want to miss this. I don't want to miss you. Your mother is no longer with us, but I want to be here for you." There's a flicker of something in my chest, then: not quite forgiveness, but maybe the beginning of it. I nod.

"Thank you, dad, I really appreciate that." My father stands and reaches for the box. I stand, too, and for a moment, we just look at each other—then we share a warm hug.

"I'm proud of you," he says.

"Thank you." For once, I feel like he's looking at me like the thirty-something-year-old adult that I am, and not the troubled teenager I used to be. Khalid steps forward and offers a light hug.

"Good meeting you, man. I know it was short, but we'll have more chances to hang out," he says, his voice hopeful, easing the tension.

"I'll look forward to that," my dad replies, a flicker of genuine excitement in his voice. As he turns and walks out the door, something settles in the air. Khalid and I slide back into our seats, and I rest my head against his arm. The air between us feels different now—calmer, lighter, like something heavy finally loosened its grip.

"How are you feeling, baby?" he asks gently.

"She told him." He blinks, surprise flashing across his face.

"Are you serious?"

"I wish I weren't. I'll never get that back. But what's done is done. Now we just focus on looking ahead. I'm not putting pressure on anything." He leans down and kisses the top of my head, and for a moment, I let myself breathe in his steadiness. It grounds me. After a few beats of silence, I glance up at him.

"How was orientation today? You're nearly done with it right?"

"Great. Easy, actually. And yeah, I'm near done. A lot of things were cut short since I'd already done most of it for my contract—now it's just finishing the permanent stuff." I nod, tracing circles on the back of his hand.

"How does it feel to be permanent? Different at all?" He shrugs, a small smile forming.

"Not really. I like it here a lot though. Everyone's real cool, leadership loves my work ethic, and James is my boy. The work's the same, but the pay's much better out here. I thought it was just the contract." I laugh softly.

"Well, that's always nice, we love the extra coin."

"It is," he says, his thumb brushing over my hand. "And it's important. With our baby on the way and getting our own space, I want to make sure we're more than set. I want you to know you don't have to carry anything but what you love. Your shop, your passions, that's yours. Let me worry about the rest." Something inside me softens at the way he says "our baby", and the gentle nudge that he wants to provide for us. It's such a simple sentence, but it hits deep. I look at him, warmth rising in my chest.

"You always say things like that so calmly, like you don't realize how big they are. I love that you want to do this for me, for us." He smiles, eyes unguarded.

"I wouldn't have it any other way. From the moment I met you, I knew it was going to be hard to stay away. As time went on, I couldn't imagine my days without you."

"You mean so much to me, Khalid," I say leaning into him as I let out a light yawn.

"Let's get you home, baby. We can take a nap together and re-watch Soul if you want."

"Hmm I'd love that," I murmur.

*

When we pull up to the house, I notice a large box sitting on the front porch.

` "Who's that from?" Khalid asks, squinting. "Amazon?"

"I'm not sure. I ordered a lot of things for our new place but I wasn't expecting anything to come today." I pick it up and carry it inside, curiosity stirring. As I open it, I find a small brown envelope tied with twine resting on top of the packaging.

I slide the note free and read Sage's familiar handwriting:

175

A small Polaroid slips from the envelope and flutters into my palm. It's Sage, glowing, her baby girl that's now a few months old bundled in her arms, both of them caught mid-laugh. My chest warms instantly and I feel my eyes get glossy. Beneath the note, I pull back the layers of packing paper to reveal a large vacuum-sealed pregnancy pillow, compressed tight to fit the box. I laugh, touched to my core. Khalid grins.

"Looks like somebody knows what you need." I trace the twine still in my hand, smiling.

"She always does."

# CHAPTER TWENTY-FIVE
## *Mia*

The morning light spills through the blinds, soft and golden, and I'm still half-asleep when Khalid leans over to kiss my shoulder.

"Come on, sleepyhead," he teases gently. "We've got an appointment."

"What time is it?" I groan.

"10:45 a.m."

I sit up and breathe as though I just ran a marathon. At thirty-nine weeks, even rolling out of bed feels like a mission. Khalid turns to me and offers his hand, I let him pull me up, grumbling under my breath as I waddle toward the bathroom.

"Don't laugh," I warn, side-eyeing him through the mirror. He grins.

"I wouldn't dare." I brush my teeth and nearly gag halfway through. For a second, I brace my hands on the counter, breathing through the wave of nausea. It passes, barely.

"Still hanging in there?" he asks from the doorway.

"Barely," I mumble, rinsing my mouth. By the time I step out, he's already waiting with a steaming cup of ginger tea. The smell alone calms my stomach.

"You're a lifesaver," I say, taking a sip. "Whew, I may just have to keep you forever."

He smirks, leaning against the dresser.

"Ain't got a choice," he says, voice low but sure. "I'm not going anywhere."

Something in the way he says it makes my heart skip—like a promise he doesn't even have to think twice about. He grabs the little glass bottle from the nightstand—the belly serum I swear by—and warms a few drops between his palms. When his hands touch my skin, I close my eyes. His thumbs trace lazy circles across my belly, the same way he does every morning, whispering prayers I can barely hear. Love words, gratitude, little promises that make my chest ache in the best way. I chuckle.

"I swear you love rubbing that serum on my belly more than I do." He grins without looking up.

"Aye, belly rubs are good luck."

"Good luck for who?" I tease. He glances up at me.

"For all of us." He finishes and presses a kiss to my belly and forehead where the scar is left from the concussion after the car accident before helping me into my dress.

"Let's grab brunch before we head in," he says. "Doctor's orders— keep mama fed." I roll my eyes, smiling.

"You just want pancakes." He grins.

"Is it a crimeeee?" he sings the song playfully in response. I crack up, shaking my head. I'll always laugh with this man and I love that for me.

"You're hilarious, bae." I slip my feet into my flip-flops.

"Give me two minutes, I want to water my plants before we leave." Khalid nods and follows me toward the sliding door. The small garden stretches along the fence—simple, still growing in, but mine. I reach for the watering can, bending slowly.

"Whew... okay," I whisper, steadying myself.

Khalid steps a little closer, ready if I need him, but letting me have the moment. I tilt the watering can, watching the soil darken, and catch sight of tiny tomatoes starting to push through. Life growing while I grow life. This feels so poetic. I straighten with a slow breath, my hand resting over the quiet flutter of our baby beneath my skin and take a look around me; the house we bought for our family. It sits in a quiet suburban street like something plucked from a dream—grand but grounded, elegant without trying too hard, slightly regal with its tall arched windows and rounded turret that gave it a castle-like look. Behind it stretches the beautiful backyard like I've always dreamed. There was still much to be done around the house, but for now, the most important things were taken care of—the hospital bag packed and ready, the bassinet built, the nursery painted and waiting for our baby's arrival, the name already chosen. Destiny ended up keeping the townhome where her boyfriend had moved in and turned half of it into an art studio. It ended up working perfectly for her.

"I used to dream about this," I murmur. "A little garden in my backyard...something that would contribute to taking care of my family one day. Soon our kiddo will be out here with me," I say, smiling at the thought.

"Yeah," Khalid says, gaze drifting across the yard. "We're going to be parents. That's wild to think about, we're going to meet our baby in the coming week or so." He pauses. "I'm getting ahead of myself but eventually I wanna put a small swing set back here."

"Oh, I love that idea," I say, heart full. Then I nudge him. "Come on—I know you're hungry. Let's go get you your pancakes."

"Don't put it all on me, babymama," he laughs. "I know you hungry, too."

"You ain't lying," I laugh, looping my arm through his.

*

When we arrive at our final doctor's appointment, the room fills with the rhythmic sound of a strong heartbeat echoing through the monitor.

As I place my hand in Khalid's, he rubs slow circles across my belly with his free hand, his thumb tracing its soft curve with admiration. "Great news—the baby's no longer breeched," she says. "Everything looks perfect. And at this point, baby could come any day now."

"Oh, thank goodness!" I say, relief threading through my voice.

"That's a relief, thank God," Khalid murmurs beside me. I laugh lightly, shaking my head.

"These Braxton Hicks contractions have been doing their big one, so I believe you. She's coming out soon." The doctor chuckles.

"Hang in there. It's been a long journey for you two, but you're almost there."

As I listen to the tiny heartbeat, something in me settles. Given everything I've been through, I never saw this for myself. Just like I never imagined owning a business or finding real peace, being truly happy always felt like some distant fairytale. But here I am—whole, loved, seen.

Becoming a mother feels less like a milestone and more like something sacred. After a journey of healing, learning how to feel safe and complete on my own, I feel as though I was preparing for this without even knowing. While I was working on myself, God was preparing the greatest love story I could ever ask for.

As we leave the office, Khalid squeezes my hand, and I feel a quiet smile in his touch.

"Let's go to the beach for the sunset," he says. "I packed a blanket in the car." I glance over at him smiling.

"You planned that?"

"Of course," he says, brushing a braid behind my ear. "We deserve one last quiet moment before everything changes." I squeeze his hand back and rest my head briefly against his shoulder as we walk to the car.

"I can't believe it's almost time," I say as Khalid opens the car door for me.

"Me neither, I've never been so excited. I thank God every day."

Khalid says, tucking another braid behind my ear.

I play "As" by Stevie Wonder in the car.

"I'm so grateful my braider could squeeze me in—I love how they came out and not having to manage my hair over the next few weeks will make things a tiny bit easier for me. I'm almost in disbelief in how we're truly all set. We have everything, probably too much between the two baby showers our friends and family threw for us.

"No for real, I kept thinking, are we even going to go through all this stuff ? Not to mention your eldest stepsister Kiana sending cleaners over was a huge help after all the unpacking between the baby showers and the moving we've been doing. Everything feels ready." Khalid adds.

I pause and think about how the lingering distance between my father and I never really changed after our conversation. Angie never apologized for gossiping about my pregnancy and telling my father before I got the chance. As for Kiana, her and her daughter Maylani came to the baby shower, which truly meant a lot to me. Maylani gifted me my breast pumps and became a part of my mom tribe without question. Kiana had always seen Angie for who she was. In time, she'd made peace with it and preserved our relationship by offering quiet, steady care that helped heal what had once felt broken, our bond has grown so much. Khalid glances at me.

"What you thinking about, babe?" I look up at him then, not realizing I got quiet for a few moments.

"So much has changed over the last few months, but no matter what, I'm grateful. For our community, the love we've been surrounded with. Everything happens for a reason. I believe that." He tilts his head toward me.

"Have I ever told you the way you hold space for gratitude, even for the small things? Always has me in awe of you." I laugh softly.

"No—but I appreciate you saying that. Moving with gratitude has carried me through life."

When we arrive at the beach, Khalid spreads out a blanket for the two of us to lay on while watching the sunset and rubbing circles on my belly.

"I've been thinking," he says quietly, "about how everything started... crazy how time flies. To think that we met nearly a year and half ago now, even though it feels like it was just yesterday." He chuckles.

"Yeah. And all that in between."

"But I also think about this moment right here," he says softly. "The quiet before everything changes. And I need you to know something." He pauses. "Loving you through this has brought me so much joy. And the blessing? My love gets to expand more as you bring our baby into this world. I want to share this for the rest of my life."

"Baby, you're going to make me cry," I whisper. "I love you so, so much." He leans in, pressing his forehead gently to mine. Then pulls back just enough and looks in my eyes.

"Mia, I'm devoted to you. In this lifetime and the next. I want my love to be vivid, abundant, and unmistakably yours—the kind that shows up in the quiet times, the hard times, and every moment in between." Then, he reaches into his pocket and pulls out a small velvet box.

"I want you to be my wife." My hands fly to my mouth.

"Khalid...Are you serious right now?" My voice comes out trembling, my eyes already filling with tears. He nods.

"Will you marry me?" His voice is low, steady, full of everything we've survived to get here. The ring glistens before I even realize I'm staring at it. An emerald-cut center stone sits in the middle, beautiful, catching every bit of light. I pull him in and kiss him slow as the tears spill down my cheeks.

"Yes," I breathe. "Yes, a thousand times."

*

Later that week, just days after saying yes to forever, my water broke. I went into labour and after several long hours later, I gave birth. We welcomed our perfect baby girl into the world. She lays on my chest, skin to skin and when she opens her eyes; they're like a galaxy. She blinks slowly, already curious, already looking at us like she knows exactly who we are. Tiny curls rest against her head, tight little spirals that feel like feathers on my chest.

I'm a mother. This is the most spiritual moment I've ever experienced. An unconditional love that runs deeper than every fiber in my being. Khalid and I hold her close. She is everything, so perfect, so beautiful, so ours. Our perfect little family.

*Amirah Muharib West.*

A princess. A warrior. A legacy.

Not just a new chapter: A new book entirely.

# Acknowledgements

To my sisters — my anchors, my mirrors, my safe places. You've seen me through everything: every storm, every version of myself I wasn't sure I'd survive. You've held me through tears, laughter, confusion, and clarity. You are proof that sisterhood is a kind of love that saves you quietly, over and over again.

To my husband — my calm in the chaos, my steady hand through every chapter of this journey. You carried me through my self-doubt and celebrated my smallest wins like they were victories. Thank you for being my best friend, my love story, and for believing in this book even when I questioned whether I could tell it.

This story comes from the deepest part of me, and I can't thank my readers enough for being here. I cried many tears writing these pages — tears of release, remembering, and gratitude. My hope is that as you read, you recognize how love shows up — not only in romantic ways, but through friendship, family, chosen people, and heart-aligned souls who remind us that love takes many forms. Additionally, something I learned in writing this story is that healing can show up in many ways—sometimes it's loud and transformative, other times it's quietly sitting with it and after navigating the stillness, choosing to keep moving forward.

This book would not be what it is without my editing team at **BGWW- Black Girls Who Write.** Working on a Black romance novel with Black women was a profound privilege. I felt held every step of the way. You all handled this story with care, honesty, and intention. Tamika — in a space where I had very little guidance and the final stages felt lost and nearly wanted to give up, you became a voice of clarity, mentorship, and reassurance in a short but powerful window of time. You encouraged me to think deeper. You told me what I needed to hear and pushed me creatively. You showed me the importance of loosening my grip on rigid timelines so the story could breathe and become the best version of itself, I can't thank you enough. I appreciate you deeply and owe so much of that growth to you. This project means so much to me, it carried me through my postpartum. I'll never forget the impact you made in this season of my life.

# About the Author

Hi. This is my first time writing an "About the Author" section, so bear with me. Somehow, this part feels harder than writing an entire novel. My relationship with writing began early. In 6th grade, I won second place in a small poetry competition at my school. A poem about my mom moving away with my sisters while I went to live with my father. I had never put those feelings into words before, the loneliness, the adjustment, it was really hard on me. Poetry quietly became my first safe place to tell the truth.

In high school, writing became something more personal. In my writing class, we were required to write short stories for the first twenty-five minutes every morning. Most people dreaded it, but it became my favorite part of the day. For my senior project, what should've been your basic final writing assignment of some off amount of pages turned into a short story about a traumatic experience I had been carrying alone. When my teacher, Ms. Lewandowski, read it, she realized the story was about me and said, "Everything you wrote and what happened to you… this could be a novel if you keep going." I never forgot her words.

As I grew older, I kept writing; journaling, taking creative-writing classes in college, and returning to the page whenever I felt myself needing it. I wrote a few short stories but nothing to this magnitude. In college, I had a random idea, I wrote a story through Facebook status posts telling people I'd only continue if the status hit 5 likes. 5 likes became 15 likes, soon, I had to raise it to 100 likes because so many people were waiting for the next part, and I needed time to create the story as I wrote. It was my first taste of sharing stories with an audience that couldn't wait to turn the "page." Years later, Unmistakably Yours began in the simplest way: by writing on the mirror in my office with an Expo marker. I started sketching out who my characters were, what they carried, how I wanted them to grow, and the kind of love I wanted them to step into. One reflection became a sentence, a sentence became a scene, and somehow an entire story bloomed.

I started writing this story when my son was just 4 months old. This is my first full-length novel — shaped by every version of me: A little girl who used poetry to survive change, A teenager finding her voice through pain, and now A mother in postpartum healing through words and finally choosing to share stories out loud. As I found my words, my son, who is now just shy of two years old, began to find his. When I'm not snuggling with my son, I'm reading, or rewatching my comfort movies — Soul, Spirited Away, Rush Hour 2... and yes, even reruns of Insecure. I'm usually tucked under my man because what can I say? I love him real bad lol, he makes me laugh constantly and just feel safe and I love that for me. If I'm not cooking or baking something, I'm dancing on the pole — my favorite mix of strength, confidence, and joy. I'm a Bay Area native and my Black identity is shaped by my Haitian heritage, and Middle Eastern roots, building a life, a family, and a new chapter as an author. I've done a lot of things in life, but this...this feels like my best work. Thank you for supporting my very first novel. It truly means more than you know.

**Stay connected!**

**Moonlightandpenpublishing.com**

**Instagram: Ninilove123**

**Threads: Ninilove123**